PRAGUE

BETWEEN HISTORY AND DREAMS

First Edition

Written and translated from the Czech by Václav Cílek
Adapted by Barbara Froula

Research Assistance
Brooke Cleary Sandoval

Editorial Assistance
Raven Moore Amerman, David Engelken, Adrienne Mullineaux, Tim Adams

Acknowledgements

In the chapter Spirit of Place, Czech poet Vítezslav Nezval's book *Prague Pedestrian* is freely cited. The title of the poem "And death shall have no dominion" by Dylan Thomas is included in the Kutna Hora chapter, because we often read this poem in the ossuary. Poet J. Halas dedicated the verse about fish in the cathedral to the memory of an outstanding Czech poet of Jewish origin, Jiri Orten, who tragically died in 1942. Besides pundit of Czech literature Petr Bilek from Prague and Neo-anarchist Jerry Zaslove from Vancouver our gratitude belongs (in spite of some communication problems) to the noble, but mostly obstinate and unobliging spirits of described places.

To order additional copies of this book, contact:
Xlibris
844-714-8691
www.Xlibris.com
Orders@Xlibris.com

ISBN: Softcover   978-1-4134-3192-6
        Hardcover   978-1-4134-5531-1

Library of Congress Control Number: 2003096984

Print information available on the last page

Rev. date: 12/07/2020

CONTENTS

THE SPIRIT OF THE CITY

Prague is one of the last great European cities where— as Ranier Marie Rilke once said— things are aware of us.

Relationships created over hundreds of years can't be easily destroyed—relationships to those complicated yet ordinary things: wood, soil, the landscape. The unique awareness in mind and heart of those things that form the essence of a place is called *genius loci*—something that cannot be given a name, but to which we always return.

In his book *Baroque Prague* (1915), Arne Novak says: "Genius loci consists of the matter of our minds and hearts, it is a spiritual reality, but its visible embodiment is place. Prague, however, belongs to those cities with a rich past that contains several genius loci of various ages and outlooks. If we focus too much on any one, the others will escape our attention. But it is possible to love the city in such a way that we devote ourselves to the genius loci of many different periods, thus enriching our lives."

Prague is a house with a thousand floors. We live on the upper four or five levels, only vaguely aware of the rest. Yet, thanks to fossils from Prokop valley, mushrooms from the Nebusice woods, and the age-old yew trees below Prague Castle, we can touch the mysteries of ancient lives and passions that have sprung from this magical place. The city reveals much of itself and keeps many secrets. We can move through it vertically—from one level to another—or horizontally, from place to place. Or we can experience it as a collection of atoms, an immense person—a living being.

Prague lies just north of the geometric center of the historic kingdom of Bohemia, which, combined with Moravia, forms today's Czech Republic. The relationship between Prague and the rest of the country is so intimate that it is impossible to understand Prague without the Czech countryside, and without knowing Prague, it is impossible to comprehend the Czech Republic. Prague is located on a spot where continuous Slavic settlement goes back to at least 650 A.D. Before that time, twenty successive ceramic cultures, each

GENIUS LOCI

Genius loci literally means "spirit of a place." In ancient Rome, spirits of a place were treated like living beings with a collective soul. It was sometimes believed that the spirit of a certain place grows and develops, or diminishes and declines, in relation to the quality of its dead. Heroes, saints, artists and other people with some message pass after death into a larger body of genius loci. Romans later recognized that not only places, but also different periods of time, may have their spirits and guardians. They are often called by the German word *Zeitgeist* (spirit of the age). The complex mythology of these ancient concepts should not hide one basic revelation: place and time are not things under our control, but mighty strangers whom you must ask for permission to know and to be known. They are the gentle, invisible and powerful hand in the background.

with its own stories, music and ornaments, flourished and then died. Twenty lost civilizations, twenty Atlantises! Their spirit and art have disappeared into time immemorial.

In Prague we are steeped in a mysterious cauldron filled with such personalities as Franz Kafka, Johannes Kepler, and Wolfgang Amadeus Mozart, minds that stirred the music, myth, and thought of the Western world. What does this cauldron contain? Maybe we can call it the Great Memory— the sum of acts, feelings, fears and hopes of past generations. We may notice suffering and adversity in this vast cauldron of collective memory, but somehow, beauty, sacrifice and love are more powerful. One has to spend some time among old walls, eat and drink in Baroque taverns and pray in centuries-old churches to realize that the Great Memory is not just another bright concept that should be studied, but part of your breath.

FOUNDATION

For years I have been walking through Prague as if through a Mexican jungle, looking for lost cities. That which is written down in the human history of Prague is also reflected in the stone at the city's feet. The foundation of Prague is a combination of the soft shale that helped create its valleys, and the resistant quartzite that forms the city's hills of Vitkov, Hrad and Vysehrad. The top layer is chiefly made up of strong, horizontal Mesozoic sandstone, porous enough to allow for the emergence of the natural springs found in several monasteries and palaces. The Vltava River flows into Prague's "cauldron" across eleven levels, corresponding to at least eleven ice ages. The Prague area thus resembles a giant natural theater with huge steps forming the rows of seats. Enchanted by the contrast of the river and the hills, architects designed such important buildings as Prague's Gothic Saint Vitus' Cathedral and Baroque Saint Nicholas' Church in mathematical proportion to the depth of the Vltava River valley. Some of the best architecture is, after all, just an extension of nature.

PRAGUE CASTLE/PRAZSKY HRAD

Resting gloriously upon a high hill and visible from anywhere in the city, the Prague Castle complex is one of the largest in Europe, representing a thousand years of Czech architecture. The buildings surrounded by the castle walls include the Picture Gallery of Prague Castle, St. Vitus' Cathedral, the Powder and Dalibor Towers, the Royal and Lobkowicz Palaces, St. George's Basilica and Convent, and Golden Lane.

FOREST

A noticeable and vital aspect of Prague is the immense, untamed forest of Petrín Hill. It is an echo from an age in which the valley below was dominated by a forest of willows and alders along the banks of the Vltava. Upslope from the river grew maples, ash trees, elms and giant oaks. The slopes of Petrín were clothed by groves of scrub oak; side gorges were home to fir and beech trees.

The arrival of human beings transformed the landscape—wild growth was replaced by fields grazed down by sheep. Even as late as the end of the 19th century, shepherds could still be seen in Letná Park, and it was not uncommon to find herds of cows making their way across Charles Bridge. Until recently, heather covered the slopes of Vítkov hill where the statue of Hussite general Jan Zizka now stands.

Over the years, exotic plants appeared in the area, along with exotic faces. Together with the Vietnamese vendors, Ukrainian workers and American fast food, we find plants from Canada, China and other countries of the Far East. All of them will stay and become part of the landscape, and why not? Was it really so long ago that woolly rhinos walked on what is now Wenceslas Square, or that baboons inhabited the Koneprusy caves not far from Prague? Place is a conduit through which history flows, representing not only numbers and dates in books, but the creation of mountains, the retreat of the sea, the way a beech grove overtakes oaks.

The Stone Age

People have lived in Europe for about a million years, and they first appeared in the area around Prague around 700,000 years ago. For most of human history, we have lived in the Stone Age: it ended 12,000 years ago; a mere 400 generations have elapsed since then. The Stone Age therefore makes up the most basic and greatest part of our consciousness. Siberian shamans existed not only in Siberia during that age, but also in the Zizkov and Jizni Mesto areas of Prague. The fields surrounding the city are still strewn with crude instruments made of quartz. For thousands of years, people have been coming down the gentle slopes around Prague into the wide river basin below. As we sit on the hills overlooking the Vltava river, we open the window of our consciousness to what the landscape can reveal—our ancestors are not as far away from us as we think.

Celtic Bohemia

The name Bohemia is derived from the Celtic tribe called Boii, who lived here until the first century A.D. Celtic tribes had settled, and perhaps originated, in the area around the Rhine and the Labe Rivers between the late Bronze and early Iron Age. At their peak, the Celtic settlements on Czech lands were even denser than the largely Slavic ones of the early Middle Ages. At the southern edge of Prague lies Závist, one of the largest Celtic settlements in Europe, with an area of 420 acres and surrounded by city walls that can be followed for eleven miles! Few medieval towns were as large as this wooden fortress. Many Czech traditions and superstitions have direct roots in this period, and Celtic hill forts remain dispersed throughout the Bohemian countryside.

BIRTH OF THE CITY

The Czechs, a Slavic tribe, settled the region and established their language in two waves during the 6th and 7th century A.D. From the end of the 9th century and into the early 10th century, the ten to fifteen villages and other settlements lying in the Prague basin began to coalesce into a larger residential area, which was likely centered on the marketplace located at today's Malá Strana Square. The steep and rather narrow hill where the castle now stands was perhaps the only one of Prague's seven hills that remained unsettled in the year 885. In that year, construction began on a fortification guarding the marketplace and the ford of the Vltava where Charles Bridge was later built.

Prague was located at the crossroads of major trade routes and on the ancient Vltava River "highway." Thanks to communication with the rest of Europe, it grew into a position of central importance. The Prague we know is the commingling of four separate historic towns—Stare Mesto, Nové Mesto, Malá Strana and later Hradcany—with the castle.

A COSMIC DIMENSION?

Another dimension, or level, of Prague is a magical, cosmic aspect inherited from primeval and Celtic times and later pursued by Gothic builders and Renaissance seers in the court of Rudolph II. It is reflected in Old Town Square's Astronomic Clock; in the activities of astronomers Johannes Kepler, Tycho Brahe, and Giordano Bruno (who used to walk around Prague Castle and say that the stars were wiser than people); in the frescoes of Valdstejn Palace; in the location of Charles Bridge; and in astrological legends.

Although currently viewed as something romantic, the primeval and Middle Ages conceptions of aligning the geometric plan of the landscape with celestial bodies were originally intended to translate cosmic order onto Earth. Why do we read sci-fi, why do we watch Star Trek or Star Wars, if not for the sense of being connected, like people of the past, to the stars and other planets?

Standing in the center of Charles Bridge under the Old Town Bridge Tower (dedicated to St. Vitus), we can observe the

sun touching the horizon on the summer solstice at exactly the place in St. Vitus' Cathedral where the altar of St. Vitus is located. If we look at a map and connect the presbyteries of Prague's Romanesque churches, such as the Basilica of St. Vitus and the rotundas of St. Kríze and St. Longinus, we discover that the sites, formerly occupied by pagan statuaries, can be connected by summer solstice lines (connecting the observer and the rising sun on the solstice). Winter solstice lines have been found to be in alignment with Romanesque churches in Chabry, Bohince, Sárka, Dolní Liboc and Repy. The churches themselves are positioned east to west; entering the church for morning mass means leaving darkness behind.

ROMANESQUE AND GOTHIC PRAGUE

Romanesque buildings and Gothic places have a special kind of memory that doesn't rely on words written in books. Churches of this early time were

often dark, cave-like sanctuaries where a person could be alone, stepping down into the inner sphere of personal salvation. By contrast, in later Baroque times, one could get outside of oneself in a well-lit church filled with people and be directed toward the salvation of the whole community.

Prague's serene beauty masks the profound fears of medieval times. I could easily slip into describing how Gothic architecture reconciles the human dimension of the body and the cosmically created universe. But instead, I'm thinking about plague and civil war, about expectations of the apocalypse and about Hussite Reformationist* attempts to hasten this end. As one becomes aware of all the suffering (sometimes meaningful, but more often useless), all the wars, the pogroms, and the malicious small-mindedness,

frightening images come to mind. Imagine this apocalyptic snapshot from 1420: late in the day, a Hussite mob marches back to Prague. Behind them on the hillside is the vast Zbraslav monastery, engulfed in flames. *(p. 64)

RENAISSANCE

The Renaissance lasted for a short period in Prague (1540–1610), leaving only a few visible traces of construction. The Renaissance laid the foundation, though, for something very modern: individualism and an extensive consumer society. Prague's Renaissance is mostly viewed through the prism of the court of Rudolf II, which hosted an array of magicians and alchemists as colorful as a Harry Potter novel. As one might imagine, there was more magic in the 16th century than in the Middle Ages.

Baroque Prague

The Baroque period was a reaction to the rationality of the Renaissance and an attempt to absolve the alleged, and actual, guilt of heresy from the Reformation. During this period and for the following 300 years, the Catholic Hapsburg dynasty controlled Bohemia, its culture and language. It was a period of grandiose buildings built with the technical perfection of the Italian masters, infused with Czech spirit. Sculptured gardens and chapels in the woods from this period sanctify the landscape and connect its archaic and cultural soul. Baroque architecture can serve as an inspiration for Europe's future, because it combines international style with regional flavor.

If you visit the Gothic cathedral of St. Vitus and then the Baroque church of St. Nicholas, you may have the feeling that they belong to two different religions. Yet the Czech soul is a fusion of the solemn, introverted Gothic and the colorful grandeur of Baroque.

Prague Today

The tourist explosion begins at 9:00 in the morning. Just after breakfast in the hotels, the city becomes inundated. The genius loci—the spirit of the ages that rises from the city, connecting you to Prague's ancient past—is trampled down deep into the cobblestones by the throngs of tourists, while the Czechs mutter, "The city is no longer ours." "Why didn't Max Brod just burn Kafka's work? Why do people without a shred of sensitivity amuse themselves at the expense of his unhappiness?" a friend says to me, pointing at one of the ubiquitous Kafka posters.

Czech life is shifting from the expensive historic center to other nearby districts, where you can find cheaper shops and better restaurants frequented by locals. Until recently, these outer districts were dependent on the historical core of the city, but today they are becoming more independent, as in the lively district of Zizkov, where you can see from one pub to another.

The Elusive Quality of Place

Prague's poetry is written in the mysterious texture of architecture and landscape, the complexity of history and myth. It's not only Prague's Powder Tower or Old Town Square or Charles Bridge or Old or New Prague, nor only the legends or beauty of Prague. It is found in the way a bird perches on the forehead of the city, the way a child calls to her mother as they pass a Baroque statue.

PRAGUE CASTLE
TALES OF POWER AND
SEARCH FOR A SNOWFLAKE

Throughout the Middle Ages, two complementary aspects of power were recognized: sacerdotium and imperium, or sacred and imperial power—the bishop and the king. The combination was necessary but dangerous, because power of any kind tends toward its own corruption and political power likes to use the church for its own purposes. Czechs have ambivalent feelings toward the Castle. On the one hand, it is the most visible and beloved symbol of the historic Kingdom; on the other, it is the seat of a central power that is as likely to be distrusted or despised as it is to be respected.

SAINT VITUS' CATHEDRAL/CHRAM SV. VITA

Prague's most characteristic landmark, St. Vitus' Cathedral, was founded by Charles IV in 1344. The building's primary architect was Petr Parlér, who influenced all of Bohemia's later Gothic architecture. Work by 19th- and 20th-century artists finally completed the cathedral by 1929. Housed here are the crown jewels of Bohemia. Architectural features not to be missed include the Golden Portal (Zlata Brana), decorated with a mosaic of the Last Judgment, and the Chapel of St. Wenceslas. The chapel houses the tomb of Czech patron saint King Wenceslas, who built the Rotunda of St. Vitus in the same location one thousand years earlier, and it is ornately decorated with frescoes and semi-precious stones. Also among the cathedral's treasures are the sword and helmet of Wenceslas and the bronze ring to which he is thought to have clung when slain by his brother Boleslav. St. Vitus' is the largest religious structure in Prague and is the seat of Prague's Archdiocese.

ARCHBISHOP'S PALACE/ARCIBISKUPSKY PALAC

Built in 1564 to replace the old Archbishop's palace (destroyed during the Hussite Wars of the previous century), the late Baroque palace *(at left, opposite)* is attributed to architect Jean-Baptiste Mathey, with later Rococo embellishments. The palace's exquisite façade overlooks Hradcany Square, and is a monumental reminder of the power of the Catholic church in Prague. Milos Forman filmed scenes of the movie Amadeus in the beautifully furnished rooms of the Archbishop's palace.

CASTLE GATE/MATYÁSOVA BRÁNA

The Castle Gate, or Matthias Gateway, was built at the Castle entrance in 1614 in the early Baroque style. During coronation processions, Bohemian kings and queens of old paraded along the Royal Route to the Castle, which began at the Gothic Powder Gate in Old Town, crossed the Charles Bridge, and ended at Matthias Gateway.

SAINT GEORGE'S BASILICA/BAZILICA SV. JIRÍ

Originally built as a basilica in 915–921 in a pre-Romanesque style, St. George's church was enlarged in the Romanesque style after a fire in 1142. It was the burial place of early Premyslid princes, including the church's founder, Prince Vratislav. Also buried here is Princess Ludmilla, grandmother of King Wenceslas and Bohemia's first female Christian martyr, who was strangled by her daughter-in-law while kneeling at prayer. The Church of St. George is a well-preserved example of early Romanesque architecture, with Baroque adaptations of the front façade. The church and adjoining convent were an integral part of the workings of the Castle complex during the Middle Ages.

The considerable size and grandeur of Prague Castle inspires awe, but its single most astonishing attribute may be continuity. In other countries governmental centers have shifted from place to place, but the Prague Castle complex has been the seat of kings, emperors and now presidents for a thousand years. Today's presidential office is two hundred yards from the long-established offices of Bohemian kings and only one hundred yards from the bedroom of Emperor Rudolph II.

At the dawn of history, any king or local governor between Persia and England was enthroned on a kingstone (king's stone) in a ritual resembling marriage. He was unified with the country and with its feminine power. The most famous kingstone is located under the medieval wooden coronation throne of the English king in Westminster Abbey. The Bohemian kingstone was possibly a natural rock emerg-

11

GOLDEN LANE/ZLATÁ ULICKA

This row of tiny houses was built after 1597 into the arches of the Castle walls to house Rudolf II's twenty-four castle guards. The original section of the castle, under which Golden Lane is nestled, was built when northern wall fortifications were constructed in 1484. Named after the goldsmiths who lived here in the 17th century, these dwellings also housed such notables as novelist Franz Kafka and Nobel Prize-winning poet Jaroslav Seifert. During the 1950s, the decaying area was restored to its original condition and became a street of booksellers, merchants and souvenir shops. You can walk across the small width of the houses and look into the upper branches of tall trees growing from the moat below.

Walking slowly down the lilliputian street, you sense that it is the home of many fables. Gustav Meyrink, author of Golem, describes a mysterious stone that appears here to seekers on foggy nights. When Jaroslav Seifert lived in Golden Lane, his old housekeeper often had to let him in late at night after he returned from the wine tavern. One winter night, he again forgot the keys; he rang the bell, and the housekeeper opened the door as usual. In the morning, his wife asked him how he got in, as the housekeeper had died earlier the previous day. They never learned who had opened the door for the poet.

RUDOLF II (1552-1612)

Rudolf II was Bohemia's fourth Hapsburg king in its long succession of foreign rulers. He was born in Vienna but moved his imperial residence to Prague in 1583. With him came an era of increased trade, flourishing arts, and a growing sophistication in culture and science that lasted until the Thirty Year War which engulfed all of Europe. Rudolf II was a great collector of European and Bohemian art, ancient religious relics, oddities of nature, and scientific instruments. During his rule, Prague's scientific and artistic communities flourished; the Renaissance was in full swing in the Golden City. Although Rudolf paid more attention to arts and sciences than to politics, a few religious reforms were enacted during his rule. Under pressure from his brother, Archduke Matthias, Rudolf II issued the "Letter of Majesty" in 1609, granting partial religious freedom to non-Catholics. This

set the stage for a Catholic backlash, and tensions between Catholic Hapsburgs and Protestant Bohemian nobles erupted in violence. Rudolf II suffered in the crisis, losing his crown and his life in 1612. Violence ensued across Prague as the Thirty Years War began in 1618. After the Battle of White Mountain on the outskirts of Prague on November 8, 1620, the Bohemian Protestant Estates were defeated and Emperor Ferdinand reinstated the Catholic clergy to their positions of power. But the war continued until 1648.

The court of Rudolf II lives on in memory as a magical time of mysterious alchemical transformation, when Golem walked the streets of Prague, hidden qualities of gemstones were examined and the first astronomers discovered the secrets of planetary orbits.

JAROSLAV SEIFERT (1900-1986)

Jaroslav Seifert, bittersweet writer from the breed of real poets who have poetry hanging over their heads like a curse, loved art, wine and women all his life. He was honored with the Nobel Prize for Literature in 1984.

A poet and journalist since the 1920s, Seifert supported Communism but later opposed the authoritarian dictatorship of Joseph Stalin. Books of his poetry appeared every few years. The poetic experiments of his early years were replaced by a poetry of almost classical outlook and themes on love, home, tears and hopes, always sublime and elegant like a folk song, and never shallow. Seifert was a sharp observer, and maybe more to protect "all beauties of the world" than to participate in any political party, he signed Charter 77, a 1977 petition against President Gustav Husak and the Communist regime.

Seifert's funeral took place in the Abbey of St. Margaret in Brevnov. The Communist regime ordered motorcycle racers to train nearby to drown out the words of the priest. After a reading of Seifert's poem about a butterfly, a real white butterfly appeared in the nave of the church, circling around the coffin, affirming the natural greatness of this poet in a way that could not be silenced.

ing somewhere in the presbytery of St. Vitus' Cathedral, or behind it at St. George's Square: the place where the sun kissed the Earth when viewed from the Old Town end of Charles Bridge on the summer solstice.

I recently dedicated to the buildings and ruins of the Castle an entire semester course, called Anima Urbis, or Soul of the City. After weeks of studying objects and their meanings, my head is full of dates, buildings, historical events. Every detail seems important, like any sentence, any gesture from a being you love. But how can we begin to approach the Castle; how can we somehow get under its skin?

St. Vitus' Cathedral in early morning may give you an experience you will not forget. Baroque architecture was designed for the multitudes, and its primary concern was the salvation of the whole community, but medieval architecture was built for God, and its primary concern was gratitude and personal salvation. So, one should enter a medieval church alone or in a small group of mutually attuned friends. In the dim and empty Cathedral, there is usually morning Mass at 7 AM. Several nuns and other people, maybe fifteen in all, gather there, and they are as one person. Standing under the Gothic vault as though in a dark cave, you are again a medieval person who knows that solitude does not mean being alone. It may be a combination of your own insignificance and even guilt, and a spark of central light born inside. Perhaps the cathedral is an echo of the act of the creation of the universe.

After five o'clock in the afternoon, most of the tourists disappear, but the Castle remains open until midnight. You can sit in the gardens behind the horse stables (Jízdárna) to watch the sun set and to see the beautifully lit Cathedral shine against the background of the darkening sky. Or, find a place behind the Cathedral and read aloud a famous chapter in Franz Kafka's novel *The Trial*, which describes the meeting in the Cathedral between Josef K. and the priest and their enigmatic discussion about the door guardian. Kafka worked for some time in a tiny house in nearby Golden Lane.

I sometimes take the tram to Pohorelec station and walk down to the Castle, turning at Loreto Square down through Cerninska Street to Novy Svet (New World). My feet like the quartzite cobblestones of Novy Svet and its small houses.

You may notice, by the Pohorelec tram station, a memorial statue of Tycho Brahe and Johannes Kepler. They had a small astronomy observatory in the garden of a nearby school. Emperor Rudolf II used to come here. Sharp-eyed Tycho Brahe was the best practical astronomer of his period, sitting over a pile of his collected astronomical observations but unable to sort it out. He lived like a knight. His house was always full and noisy, and he loved wine and good company. Johannes Kepler was the opposite—his weak eyes prevented him from observing the stars. His irregular salary was one-tenth of Brahe's, and he sent most of his money to his wife. He loved humble evenings spent in solitude over mathematical

THE LORETO/LORETA

Prague's Loreto (*above*) houses the Santa Casa, a reproduction of a house believed to be the Virgin Mary's, and has been an important pilgrimage center for more than 300 years. It was commissioned by founder Katerina Lobkowicz in order to spread the legend of the Santa Casa revelation: At the house of the original Santa Casa, now located in the small Italian village of Loretto, the Archangel Gabriel was said to have spoken to Mary about the impending birth of Jesus. The Loreto's elaborate construction was motivated by Ferdinand II's desire to recatholicize the Czechs. Architect Giovanni Battista Orsi designed the Baroque building in 1626–1631, and it was completed by other artists and by Christoph and Kilian Ignaz Dientzenhofer in 1661. Inside the cloistered enclosure of the Prague Loreto is a courtyard surrounded by the Loreto Treasury, which holds the famous host monstrance decorated with 6,222 diamonds; the Church of the Nativity; and the Santa Casa reproduction in the center of the complex. Positioned around the complex are the chapels of St. Joseph, St. Francis, St. Ann, St. Anthony, and the chapel of Our Lady of Sorrows.

formulae. He was not so much interested in astronomy as in harmonia mundi, harmony of the universe. His mind was sharp, he was the best theoretician of his era, and, in a house at the end of Charles Bridge, he discovered his two first laws of planetary orbits—the greatest scientific accomplishment ever made in Prague. Space travel, cell phones, and global positioning devices are all directly linked to this discovery.

Is the world established on some simple general mathematical principles according to which God built the universe? Kepler spent most of his life contemplating these questions. The search for the number six is described in Kepler's book, *Six-Cornered Snowflake*, which marked the beginnings of scientific crystallography. One winter afternoon, walking down from a meeting with the emperor at the Castle, he observes the snowflakes falling onto his coat and counts the corners. There are always six. He asks himself, why six and not five or eight? Which principle selected the number six from all possible numbers? He speculates on the soul of the Earth—does it have it a cubic form, since a cube has six planes? Does this soul project its shape and the number six through the water vapor to form snow, influencing everything under Heaven?

This is just one of the stories Prague is made of. They still hang in the air. It is so natural and innate to walk the same streets discussing some basic principles of Earth systems and behavior without noticing that we are repeating the same questions asked four centuries ago by Kepler. Like a Renaissance echo, we may ask: Is the world a mathematical machine moving in cycles and thus predictable? Or is it an immense organism, a higher animal, and thus, like any other being, unpredictable? As we face global change, the questions and answers seem as real and eternal as ever.

MIHULKA TOWER/VEZ MIHULKA

During the reign of King Vladislav II, architect Benedict Ried built this tower *(above)* as a cannon bastion on the northern wall of the castle, overlooking the stag moat. The 1496 Gothic tower, destroyed by fire in 1541, was rebuilt as the house of Tomás Jaros, maker of Prague's largest bell at St. Vitus' Cathedral. In the late 16th century, the Powder Tower became Rudolf II's alchemy laboratory. It was here that innovators like Edward Kelley conducted experiments that persuaded the emperor that it was possible to transmute lesser metals into precious gold. The tower serves as a museum relating to Jaros' bell foundry and the history of alchemy. The museum also exhibits arts and crafts of the Renaissance, and developments in science and technology under Rudolf II.

CAPUCHIN MONASTERY/KAPUCÍNSKY KLASTER

This former monastery and garden complex *(left)* is the oldest Capuchin monastery in Bohemia. Built in 1600–02, it includes the Church of Our Lady of Angels and is linked to the Loreto by a raised gangway. The monastery's architecture reflects the asceticism and simplicity valued by the Capuchin order. A monk from this order invented a style of coffee called cappuccino.

NEW WORLD/NOVY SVET

Novy Svet *(next page)*, nestled close to Prague Castle in Hradcany, was largely occupied by castle workers during the 14th century. Although inhabited by poorer members of society, the modest masonry and stucco houses and shops were an important part of the Golden City, as shown by some of their names: "The Golden Acorn," "The Golden Pear." Most of the well-preserved structures date from the 1600s. The idyllic neighborhood is known for attracting Prague's artistic and intellectual community.

VYSEHRAD
GATE OF A MYTH

Past and present, and something even more ancient, mingle in the sacred earth of Vysehrad, a refuge for those whose feelings are as important as their knowledge. It is not clear what can happen here on the ancient route from the reliquaries of the saints buried in the Castle, across the river, to the keys of Paradise held by Saint Peter in Vysehrad. I am not even sure if meditation on these matters is the best approach to understanding. I would rather sit on the steps of the Saint Wenceslas statue in Vysehrad and wait for a grey figure, and look deeply into his eyes; I know of nothing we could tell each other in words.

Vysehrad is the fortress that guarded Prague from attacks from the south. A Slavic settlement was established here after 800 A.D. on the ruins of several prehistoric sites dating back to the Chalcolithic period of the 25th century B.C. The name Vysehrad literally means "high castle," or "acropolis," referring both to the prominence of the fortified rock and the site's sense of being noble and sacred. The ancient fortress was largely destroyed during the Hussite Wars, and a new fortress was built here after the Thirty Year War, yet Vysehrad represents more than a military base—it is an anchor for the Czech national spirit. It is a Prague memorial that is visited mostly by local people, a place where you must feel more than can be seen.

Whereas Prague Castle represents the power of kings and the revered St. Wenceslas, Vysehrad is a place of legend and myth. One lives and dies for the Castle, but one sings and tells tales of Vysehrad. The Castle ghosts are connected with saints

17

VYSEHRAD

Situated on a high-walled rock outcrop overlooking the Vltava River, Vysehrad, or "castle on the hill," is a symbol of Czech national heritage as well as an important historical monument. Vysehrad comprises a park, a National Cemetery, the Church of St. Peter and Paul, St. Martin's Rotunda and excavated foundations of the ancient castle that stood here. It was from this strategically located, well-defended fortress/castle complex that the earliest Czech royalty exercised their power. Although archaeologists have not found the legendary castle of Libuse, it is believed that Princess Libuse and her husband Premysl ruled from this site. Princess Libuse is said to have stood on the hill facing the Vltava to proclaim her prophetic vision of the future glory of Prague. The fortress was damaged in several wars and demolished in 1866, leaving only remnants of the 14th-century fortifications built by Charles IV.

SAINT MARTIN'S ROTUNDA

The Rotunda of St. Martin *(right)* is a well-preserved Romanesque chapel built in the second half of the 11th century. It is Prague's oldest rotunda, restored in 1878, and is one of three surviving from the Romanesque period; Holy Rood and St. Longinus are the others. All three have naves measuring only twenty feet in diameter.

and politicians, with auguries related to the nation's destiny, but Vysehrad's ghosts just barge into the world, case lasses and make faces at the verger. The path to the Castle is paved with grave and thick historical books, but Vysehrad is more often the subject of poetry. Without Vysehrad, the Castle would not be complete—the inspiration to finish its cathedral (which legends claimed would revive the Bohemian Kingdom) was born in this place. Vysehrad is like a site from a Nordic saga, and although it is claimed that it stands at the beginnings of Czech history, it embodies not the celebrated history of a nation, but its heroic glory. The emotions Vysehrad emanates are too subtle to be harnessed in a strictly patriotic frame.

Vysehrad stands like the magician Merlin at the interface of ancient myth and the beginnings of history. Why did revivalists and patriots covet a place that more closely resembles a Late Chalcolithic settlement or Celtic shrine than a Slavic seat? I can answer only for myself: the Czech nation, like any other nation, is just a graft on an ancient tree, a tree so mighty that a weak nation seeks its support, and, only once it has become stronger, is ready to stand on its own.

Three times in Czech history, Vysehrad has played this crucial symbolic role: The first was at the end of the first millennium, when Mid-European lands underwent a process of ethnogenesis and individual tribes or extended tribal families started to consider themselves to be part of a bigger whole: a rudimentary nation. The second occasion was during the Czech National Revival of the 19th century when Slavín was established; the third was on November 17, 1989, when a group of students marching from Vysehrad were brutally stopped by police at Narodní Street—and the Velvet Revolution, which rescinded forty-one years of Communism, began.

A PLACE OF GLORY

The cemetery called Slavín (Place of Glory) was established in Vysehrad after 1875. Some of the most beloved figures of Czech culture are buried here: Bozena Nemcová, Karel Hynek Mácha, Alphonse Mucha, Bedrich Smetana, Antonín Dvorák and many others.

The 19th century was a time of rising patriotism and nationalism in many parts of Europe. Bohemia was at that time a part of the Austrian Empire, and Czechs who wanted to express their national character had very limited opportunity to do so in a military or political way. The field of culture, however, was wide open for such nationalist expression. During this time, the Czech nation rediscovered and began to nurture its language, music and cultural identity, which had been in danger of vanishing entirely due to suppression after centuries of Hapsburg domination. In the Austrian Empire, German was the language of state bureaucracy, army and business—it was the ticket to join the growing middle class. The Czech language, previously used mostly by farmers, was rather miraculously revived during this time by German-speaking intelligentsia of Czech origin, some of whom first had to learn it themselves.

This Czech Nationalism movement was based on events surrounding the French Revolution of 1789. European culture has always believed in a Story that unites. For centuries, it was the story of the Bible, the feeling that everyone is basically a child of God, that kept societies somewhat cohesive. However, during the French Revolution, this unifying story was replaced by the concept of the venerable nation. The Temple of all Gods, or Pantheon, was built in Paris as a burial place for major French writers and poets. It served as the crystallization point for the new national identity: Who am I? I am a member of a nation that has these famous writers, artists, poets and composers. The national consciousness was embodied in the bringing together of these notable personalities.

One nationalistic movement often inspires another. The Germans built Valhalla close to Regensburg (1830–1842) as a temple of German virtues, a national crystallization point. Czech nationalism followed—Slavín was the result—and the effect continued to Slovakia and other, mostly eastern European, countries.

Slavín is an outdoor museum of burial statues and of Neoclassicist and Art Nouveau ornamentation. Here you can meet Czechs who, slightly melancholy, wander around, silently reading tombstone inscriptions and falling into the vistas of the lives of those buried there, lives that are so closely associated not with successful wars and great elections, but with concertos heard, books read.

ANCIENT STONES AND SPIRITS

The oldest layer of Vysehrad can be witnessed at the foundations of the pre-Romanesque St. Laurencius Church, situated near the small beer garden. After having a beer or coffee, request a key and walk into the dimly lit basement, where you can see the unadorned foundations of three small churches situated over each other. This ancient level of the fortress is the most basic one. Just atmosphere, nothing that can be easily described, no flashes from the sky; old stones are here, and that is all.

SLAVÍN AND THE DEVIL'S COLUMN

During the 19th century, Vysehrad was turned into a monument honoring Czech culture and history. Designed in 1869–1893 by A. Wiehl, the Vysehrad Cemetery, or Slavín, is the resting place for many Czech scientific and cultural celebrities. Standing outside the cemetery gate is the Devil's Column, a mysterious stone formation that, according to legend, was left here by the devil after losing a bet with a priest. Vysehrad Park (established in 1842) lies on the west side of the monument and features stone statues by Josef Myslbek.

19

Still, I am haunted by the memory of an afternoon when, sitting behind the Romanesque Rotunda of St. Martin, my students became riveted, sensing some powerful presence there; silently fascinated, they refused to move from its grounds. We felt a connection to the genius loci of past millennia filling our souls, quenching a long-forgotten thirst. We were talking about a cold, blue light that has sometimes been seen surrounding the rotunda, a structure known, due to its antiquity, as a pagan chapel; about the Devil's column, brought by the Devil from Rome; about John the Baptist, the ruler of elements; and about the axis mundi or central axis of one of many existing worlds.

Something ancient in Vysehrad inspires this kind of experience. Nothing I would be able, or allowed, to discover, nothing I could explain, has happened to me here (well, just once I heard a mythical horse's call). But I shall be returning to Vysehrad for the rest of my life.

PRINCESS LIBUSE (700?-765?)

From the depths of ancient memory and modern imagination springs the legend of Princess Libuse, matriarch of the Czech tribe and founder of Prague. According to mythology, Libuse was the ruler of a West Slavic tribe living in the Vltava river valley around 700 A.D. As their numbers grew along with their territorial power, clansmen unhappy with having a woman as their ruler looked for a change in leadership. The far-seeing Princess Libuse forestalled any unrest by marrying a farmer of unusual strength and moral integrity, Premysl the Plowman, and making him prince of the Czechs.

The significance of her choice is better understood in the context of the many Indo-European legends in which the king plows the first furrow of the sacred field, opening the earth to the penetrating rays of the sun. The ritual was sometimes a part of a sacred marriage between a man and woman, as sky and Earth commingled in the fields to ensure their fertility. The plow also had significance in ancient towns such as Rome, which were established by a king who plowed the furrow where the city walls were be placed. The king would lift the plow from the Earth and carry (portage) it across the location of the future city gateways, or portals.

After their marriage, Libuse, according to the chronicler Cosmas, told her husband to search out a small settlement at a location she foresaw on the banks of the Vltava river and to found a city there. Premysl went to the place in Libuse's vision, where he came upon a man making a threshold or práh for his dwelling. According to legend, Libuse, Premysl and their court moved to Vysehrad, where they built a large fortress and castle which they named Praha. The 10th-century ruins at the site today are remnants of stone foundations of a later complex, one that possibly replaced Premysl's original earth-walled structures. From this rocky outcrop, Libuse prophesied the impending glory of the future city of Prague.

After Libuse died and men took over the rule over the land, a group of independent women, with a leader named Vlasta, established a castle just across from Vysehrad. They named it Devín or Maiden Castle. They were victorious over men in an attack they launched from this site in the "Maiden War". This legendary episode ended in peace, but during the next millennium the memory of these brave women was often evoked to remind men to be careful in dealings with delicate yet strong women.

Regardless of whether her story is closer to myth or fact, the social and national significance of Libuse rivals even the extreme historical significance of her dynasty. Her story is that of the Czech people. The opera Libuse by Smetana is played at the most important national celebrations. Libuse represents a historical and cultural link to the land, a spirit of independence and sense of national pride.

ST. WENCESLAS (VÁCLAV) (899?-935)

Prague's first ruling dynasty, the Premysl family, was said to be founded by the legendary princess Libuse and her consort Premysl. One of the dynasty's earliest princes was Wenceslas, who later became the honored patron saint of the Czech people. The martyred prince was entombed in the ancient Rotunda of St. Vitus (the site of today's Chapel of St. Vitus) along with his sword and helmet, which are revered relics. A manuscript dating

from the year 1006 recorded the venerable life and murder of Wenceslas as he was waylaid upon entering the church for morning Mass.

Riots and political demonstrations still take place in Václavske namesti under the statue of Saint Wenceslas as if before the only true ruler of the Czech lands. Here, the American president rang the bell of freedom after the Velvet Revolution, and here, the Dalai lama came to pay homage to the saint. The coronation crown of Bohemian kings rested on Wenceslas's skull to signify that governance is only on loan to mortal man.

Václav was killed by his brother Boleslav in a small but, at that time, important fortified center 15 miles east of Prague, now called Stara Boleslav. Václav and Boleslav are both historical figures. Both of their names mean "greater glory". So many empires, including Rome, or even realms of American Pueblo Indians, were founded by two brothers of nearly identical names. The first brother is usually a kind of a priest who establishes the spiritual rules. He is then killed by the other brother who is jealous for power but mighty enough to unify the empire and conquer its enemies. Myth is often more powerful than history, relived not only in legends and fairy tales, but in real life.

Malá Strana

Malá Strana is a quarter of delicate contrasts, stretching from the Venice of Prague—narrow streets curving along a channel of the Vltava—to the heights of Petrín Hill, a vast wooded area. It is a place for lovers and poets. After walking across the busy Charles Bridge, you stop at one of the many quiet taverns to drink in your wine and the eyes of your companion. Darkness is coming; the blackbird's ambient song rises above the noise of the traffic. As the trees of Petrín prepare for night, you can almost feel what the forest thinks. You walk up the hill like the ladder of Jacob and leave everyday life down below. Ideas creep into your mind—maybe about love, maybe about the grace of God, as tasty as the dry white wine from Melník vineyards that you sipped a while ago. The city appears below as a cauldron of light, and you are far from its madness and close to its prayers. And you walk even higher and find there not ecstasy, but the stop for the No. 22 night tram and a few noisy drunks. You are almost grateful that you can return home and leave the angelic sphere behind, because it is so beautiful to visit the realm of compassion, and so difficult to live there.

tions of the European west, or across the Balkan mountains and the rivers of Russia, from the famous Silk Road and its colorful and wealthy Oriental empires. The major north-south connection was the Vltava River, and Prague was located at one of a limited number of fords along its length.

More than a thousand years ago, Arabian and Jewish merchants frequented a large marketplace at what is now Malostranské (Lesser Town) Square, close to this ford of the Vltava River at the current location of Charles Bridge. The richness of the land and its favorable location contributed to the significance of this market. Clothes, tin ore, slaves and food are mentioned in the oldest written sources as being the principal goods available during the 9th and 10th centuries. Around 875 A.D., a wooden castle guarding the place was established at the hill above the market, giving birth to a complex that later became known as Prague Castle.

Malá Strana was for centuries the calmest of the sections of Prague. The area was occupied by palaces and houses of Czech aristocracy and foreign craftsmen—especially Italians.

Malá Strana can be viewed as a triangle of three power

Nestled below the grandeur of Prague Castle and dominated by the towers of St. Nicholas Church, Malá Strana, or Little Quarter, is a labyrinth of steep, narrow lanes, tranquil gardens, and the cool, green contrast offered by the beloved, expansive woods of Petrín Hill. The quarter of 16th- and 18th-century Renaissance and Baroque palaces, picturesque red-tiled roofs and sandstone statues overlays a more ancient history that tells of the real beginnings of the town.

Prague's location at the intersection of two vital merchant routes established its prominence over many centuries. The route brought merchants and travelers through Prague from the relatively advanced—but still barbarian—civiliza-

AT THE TWO SUNS/U DVOU SLUNCU

Along Malá Strana's idyllic Nerudova Street, which leads up to Prague Castle, many houses are known mainly by their descriptive heralds and emblems. Prior to 1770, Prague's houses were distinguished only by their unforgettable, colorful names. One such house on this well-known street was home to the Czech national poet and writer, Jan Neruda (1834-1891). The house, "At the Two Suns," (number 47) was Neruda's abode between 1845-1857. The original Renaissance house with surviving portal was built in the 16th century and was renovated in 1673-1690 with Baroque adaptations.

spots. The top corner is occupied by Strahov monastery, the right corner is the Augustinian monastery of St. Thomas where a famous dark beer (even monks must have an income) is still prepared and cheerfully consumed, and the left corner is occupied by the massive fortified Commandery of St. John of Jerusalem.

SPIRITUAL FORTRESS

As the central landmark of Mala Strana, the Church of St. Nicholas embodies a strange story comprising Jesuit ideology and the Baroque multimedia effect: architectonic grandeur, vibrating organ music and the heavenly smell of incense rising up to the church's dome. Everything is so beautiful and astonishing that one does not have time or wish to pray here. We come here to be pulled into the vortex of life—to participate in Theatrum Mundi, Theater of the World—but for private prayer, we retreat to some other more remote and humble church.

The original parish church of St. Nicholas stood in the natural center of Lesser Town as early as 1283; centuries later, after the Thirty Years War, Jesuits decided to build on the site. The founder of the Jesuit order—Ignatius of Loyola—was originally a general who fought to protect Western civilization against invading Islamic armies. Due to the military background of their founder, Jesuits conceived buildings as spiritual fortresses, occupying the most strategic places in the town

SAINT NICHOLAS CHURCH/KOSTEL SV. MIKULÁSE
This monumental Baroque church with cupola and tower was built between 1703 and 1755. Christoph and Kilian Ignaz Dientzenhofer designed the main structure, presbytery, and cupola (1703–1735), and the bell tower was built by Anselmo Lurago in 1755. Mala Strana's St. Nicholas Church is the unrivaled masterpiece of the Dientzenhofers, who did not live to see the completion of their last great monument. Magnificent ceiling frescoes depict the Celebration of the Holy Trinity. The Church of St. Nicholas has a Baroque organ that was played by Wolfgang Amadeus Mozart (1756–1791). Four days after his death, four thousand people attended a requiem Mass for him at this church.

organism. It is no coincidence that both ends of the Charles Bridge, which was for 500 years the only crossing of the Vltava in Prague, are controlled by Jesuit buildings: Klementinium College at the Old Town end of the bridge, and, at the Lesser Town end, the high green cupola of St. Nicholas Church.

Most of us tend to think about our future in the time span of maybe four to six years, as though it were determined by economists, banking interests, or trends in stock markets, but Ignatius, planning two centuries ahead, ventured at great risk but with considerable success into providing education to the more flexible minds of children as a means of influencing politics. Ironically, the Jesuits' successful accumulation of power and involvement in politics led, just a few years after the major Church of St. Nicholas was completed, to the pope's dissolution of this mighty order.

The construction of the whole Baroque complex of St. Nicholas, including the school and parish building, took place between 1673 and 1752. Renowned master builders such as Dominico Orsi and, after 1702, Christoph and Kilian Ignaz Dientzenhofer, completed the construction of one of Prague's outstanding landmarks. The church is now considered to be one of the finest examples of European High Baroque architecture. The interior is surprisingly homogeneous; almost nothing has been added or taken away since the second half of the 18th century. Dramatic character, expressiveness, plasticity of walls and careful play of light and shadow, emphasized by illusory frescoes, are major characteristics of this stimulating space.

The church's high, robust dome and thin tower may be forerunners of the more modern architecture exhibited in Prague's Dancing House (known as "Ginger and Fred"). They are a couple, more the work of a sculptor than that of an architect. The dome belonged to the church, but the thin clock tower —the tower intended to allow a lookout to give early warning when fire or an enemy threatened—belonged to the municipality. The architects, working for two different building owners, had to reconcile these contradictory forces in one building. Observing the prominent towers from different viewpoints, the eye never tires of searching for some secret relationship in their silhouettes.

The interior of St. Nicholas Church is dramatic and well designed to astonish visitors. The psychology of space is an extraordinary one. We walk through the central nave and observe how the interior affects us. The statues, with theatrical gestures, invite us inward to the presbytery. The statues grow larger and larger as we move forward, and as a result we feel increasingly smaller and more humble. But it is not the grace of the Lord nor his compassion that is making us feel smaller, but his power, his ability to destroy enemies of the church. Three different saints stand over figures of ancient fallen pagan gods or of the devil himself, displaying not love and tolerance, but violence. Large horizontal ledges hang above our heads, so we instinctively feel endangered. We may observe under the pulpit a strange pink shape resembling a marine animal or even some internal organ of the human body. Is it an alien?

The white and gold statues stand before artificial marble polished into numerous reflective patches. There is even a complex mirror located behind the central statue of St. Nicholas. Flickering candlelight renders the space even more luminous and full of motion, an effect used much later in the mirror balls of contemporary techno dance houses. The result is that our

St Nicholas church Mala Strana Prague
Mozart played the organ here 3/ 98

Nicholas belonged among the most important saints of the Middle Ages for a simple reason: according to medieval legend, he gave bread to starving children. And what parent would not be moved, in the face of his or her own hungry child, by this saint?

Saints have for a long time been an indispensable part of a social security system. People believed that their fate or the smile on their child's face could depend on their personal relationship to a specific saint. For centuries, there was a yearning to win the awareness of something transpersonal and trans-human, a touch of heaven.

An interesting feature of the modern age is that we no longer relate to saints, but there seems to be more interest than ever in angels. Saints are associated with a specific religion, but angels seem to be older than any religion and more universal, appearing under different names not only in various religions but in common dreams as well.

DEVIL'S STREAM & KAMPA ISLAND/CERTOVKA & KAMPA

Connected by a stone bridge to Malá Strana's Maltese Square, Kampa Island (below) is separated from the bank by a Vltava tributary, the Certovka, or Devil's Stream. Named after a hot-tempered noblewoman who lived in Maltese Square during the 19th century, the Certovka created an island of peaceful parks and gardens. Prior to a fire in Malá Strana in 1541 there had been no structures on Kampa, but after the 16th century fire, debris and masonry rubble was hauled to Kampa to reinforce the ground, making the island secure enough to build on. High water has covered its streets more than once (look for a marker on a house by the bridge and water wheel).

eyes have difficulty focusing on shape, as golden statues composed of shadows and reflections shimmer in the broken light. Invisible light coming from beyond, shining through visible things; coming closer to the Creator through things created—and through death and suffering—this is the Baroque concept. A difficult place is this church; we want to run away from its formidable religious ideology demanding so much.

Still, we remain because here, as in all of Bohemia, treasures are hidden that are often not mentioned in guidebooks—such as the left side altar with the small black statuette of Our Lady, miraculously found inside a fallen tree near Foy in Belgium centuries ago. It is the smallest and least beautiful statue in this church, but this is the only place in the building where we expect miracles.

We are ready to leave, but at the doorstep we hesitate for a moment, having experienced here a different aspect of life, an entire opera of religious feeling.

A SACRED OBJECT

Nearby, the Church of Our Lady of Victory in Mala Strana has a world-famous small wax statuette of Little Jesus of Prague at a side altar. The statuette is considered one of the most sacred religious objects of Bohemia.

The Little Jesus came to Prague from Spain sometime after 1555 as a wedding gift. It was donated to the church in 1628 during the Thirty Years War. In 1639, the Swedish general Banner was planning an attack against Prague. In every church in Prague, monks were praying day and night and the Carmelites held special services in front of the altar with Infant Jesus. The small figure had previously been known to help people who had prayed before it, but this time it was asked to save an entire city. Just a few days before the attack, Banner unexpectedly withdrew his armies. The rumor was that a secret messenger visited and threatened him with some unknown disaster. A similar event occurred two years later

near Regensburg, where Carmelites were praying in front of the copy of Infant Jesus. In both cases, people attributed the armies' withdrawal to the Son of God, mediated via the small wax statue.

Copies of Little Jesus were exported by missionaries to Mexico and other countries. What is considered so miraculous about the image of the boy Jesus? Is it the transformation of a small, vulnerable child into a mighty King? The poetic image of a little boy traveling through a perilous world who overcomes danger and obstacles by gentleness and forgiveness was as powerful in Prague as among the Indians of Mexico. Here we are touching what is perhaps the biggest strength and the biggest weakness of Catholicism—it is so impregnated with ancient imagery that one wonders if this kind of religion is a new form of paganism or a vast pool of sacredness where everyone can catch a fish of his or her own.

But other things in the Church of Our Lady of Victory seem out of place. At the main altar, cannons, rifles, spears and military flags surround a small icon of Our Lady that was instrumental in the victory won in the 1620 Battle of White Mountain. If such an altar were built today, would it depict tanks, cruise missiles and a Stealth bomber?

I bring students here to talk about the concept of jihad, of religious wars in Christianity. Yes, we abandoned the religious war ethos one or two centuries ago, but this wisdom was achieved only after vast suffering. One-third to two-thirds of the European population perished in the Thirty Years War (compared to six percent in W.W.II). More than a century was required for the devastated land and population to return to its pre-war state.

History's gift to us is that it may help us understand the present and anticipate that which is to come.

MALTESE SQUARE & STATUE OF ST. JOHN THE BAPTIST/ MALTEZSKE NAMESTI
Maltese Square *(above)* was named after the Priory of the Knights of Malta, which used to dominate this section of Mala Strana. The magnificent Baroque palaces lining the square were adapted in the 17th and 18th centuries by the many Catholic nobles who moved into existing townhouses. The grand Baroque Nostitz Palace (1650s) is home to the Ministry of Culture, and the Rococo Turba Palace (1767) houses the Japanese embassy. The statue of St. John the Baptist and Three Angels is prominently situated in Maltese Square among a grouping of sculptures. Ferdinand Brokof created the statuary commemorating the end of a plague epidemic. The artist shaped the face of one of the angels after his own likeness.

CERNÍN PALACE/CERNÍNSKY PALÁC

Cernín Palace *(above)* was built in 1669–1677 by architect Franceso Caratti, and from 1677–1697 by Giovanni Battista Maderna, Anselmo Lurago and others, in the Prague Baroque style. It is one of the most important examples of Baroque palace architecture in Prague. Originally built for Count Cernín, the imperial ambassador to Venice, the monumental, almost overpowering structure sits atop one of Prague's highest hills. Its massive front facade, with stucco pyramids protruding from the surface and angry faces topping its 30 Corinthian columns, inspires awe rather than admiration.

Days after the Communist Coup of 1948, the popular foreign minister Jan Masaryk, son of the first president of Czechoslovakia, was found dead following a fall from a window of the palace. There was evidence of a struggle in his apartment in the top floor of the building. He had been the only non-communist in the new government.

STRAHOV MONASTERY/STRAHOVSKY KLASTER

A steep stairway *(opposite)* leads to the monastery near the top of Petrin Hill *(left)*, which includes the Baroque Entrance Gateway (1742), the Church of St. Roch (1602–1612) and the Church of Our Lady. The Strahov Monastery contains an expansive library collection that is world famous for its age, size and cultural importance. Among its many priceless manuscripts, the museum displays a well-preserved, exquisitely decorated gospel book dating from the late 9th century. The monastery complex exemplifies Prague's architectural history. Its Romanesque core was enlarged in Gothic times, a new church was added during the Renaissance, and then the whole complex was rebuilt in the Baroque period. Many layers, one architectural being.

CHARLES BRIDGE
ON CONNECTING TWO
DIVERSE BANKS

A bridge is a unique gathering of sky and earth, divine and mortal. Where can we be more keenly aware of the intermingling of earth—represented by massive Cretaceous sandstone of the bridge pillars, of the sky full of gulls, and of the waters silently flowing under our feet? To complete the set of the Four Elements, we need only imagine the celebrations of St. John of Nepomuk: fire reflecting in the waters from torches lit at night, while music playing on boats echoes from both banks of the river.

CHARLES BRIDGE/KARLUV MOST

The Charles Bridge has spanned the Vltava River since it was built by Emperor Charles IV in 1357 to replace the flood-damaged Judith Bridge (1148-1324). Built by Petr Parlér and completed in 1402, the bridge contains 31 monumental statues of saints dating from the 17th through the 20th century. The truce that ended the Thirty Years War was signed in the middle of the bridge in 1648. The magnificent Gothic Old Town Tower has retained its original appearance since the 14th century. On the opposite side of the river stands the Mala Strana Towers. The smaller, Romanesque (Judith Bridge) Tower was originally built in the 12th century, and was adapted in the Renaissance style in 1591. The larger Mala Strana Tower was built in 1464, and the two are connected by a gateway over the entrance to the bridge.

CHARLES IV

After Premysl I unified the Czech lands in 1212 into a powerful central European state, Bohemia was granted international recognition. However, with the death of his successors in 1306, the male line of the Premyslid dynasty ended. Following the crisis, Duke John of Luxembourg (who had married Elizabeth, the younger daughter of Wenceslas II) and his Czech supporters laid claim to the Bohemian throne. Charles IV (baptized Wenceslas) succeeded the German throne, and upon the death of John of Luxembourg, became the ruler of the Bohemian kingdom. The growing supremacy of the Bohemian seat overwhelmed the neighboring German imperial territories, and while France and England crumbled under the Hundred Years' War, Charles IV acquired several important regions across central Europe.

With the territorial expansion, growing wealth, and the resulting importance of the Czech capitol of Prague, the powerful Bohemian Empire enjoyed a flourishing economy and relative stability. At the height of his glory, Charles IV elevated Prague to the imperial seat and capital of the Holy Roman Empire. The building boom during his reign produced St. Vitus' Cathedral, Charles Bridge, the development of New Town, and the foundation of a significant university, duly named Charles University, in 1348.

Charles Bridge is a happy fusion of technology and utilitarian function with the highest level of art evident in both its design and in the museum of Baroque statues standing on its pillars. Here, the sacred and the profane interact to create a powerful image. The bridge seems to rise up as naturally as the trees on the banks. The relationship between bridge and river is a harmonious (albeit stormy, during high floods) marriage. The river has the freedom to flow unfettered by the structure, while the bridge firmly connects both banks.

The chief builder of the bridge, Petr Parlér, was the same architect who built and carefully planned St. Vitus' Cathedral. He never worked randomly; there was always a symbolic and mathematical calculus behind his projects.

A certain irregularity in both the height and alignment of the bridge contributes to its beauty. It rises from Old Town, then lowers towards the Mala Strana side, bending along its length and slightly angled against the river's flow to fortify its base against the ice that piles against the bridge in late winter. The bend was an important defensive measure: a shot from one end of the bridge could not reach the other end.

The bridge itself is 520 meters long, 10 meters wide, and rises some 7 meters above the river; it has 16 arches and 17 pillars. It was built at the location of a former ford, where as early as the end of the 9th century a wooden bridge already stood. Such bridges had been quite common since ancient times, when Roman legions used a unified wooden construction that could be easily dismantled during fights or during winters and floods. The wooden bridge was replaced in 1169–1171 by a wonder never seen before—the stone bridge of Queen Judith. When that bridge was damaged by floods, King Charles commissioned the Prague (or Stone) Bridge, which, centuries later, was named after him. For more than five centuries, it was the only bridge in Prague and one of very few bridges rising above the Vltava over its entire course. Walking over the bridge, you share the same space as every Bohemian king, queen, poet, university master, heretic and hangman.

JOHN OF NEPOMUK

The most famous and the oldest (1683) statue on the bridge is the bronze statue of the martyred St. John of Nepomuk (Jan Nepomucký). In 1393, this vicar of the Prague diocese was arrested and tortured as the result of quarrels between king Wenceslas IV and the Prague archbishop. The king could not attack the archbishop directly, but he could arrest and torture his secretary and church lawyer, John of Nepomuk. John died during interrogation.

His body was thrown into the Vltava from Charles Bridge close to a place where his statue now stands. And the rest is the sort of myth that is usually more powerful than history: A drought came, which dried the Vltava river. Five sparkling stars appeared above the place where the body of the martyr was found. People believed in the sanctity of John of Nepomuk, and those who did not believe still found a reason to blame the king. A legend grew about a priest named John who refused to tell the king the secrets he learned from the queen in the confessional. John became a secret patron saint of the Czech nation until he was canonized in 1729 as a martyr of the tongue. When he was canonized, his remains were excavated from a tomb in St. Vitus' Cathedral, and a pink substance was found in the skull. It was believed that it must be the tongue of the martyr. Later it was proved that it was, in fact, a piece of his brain soaked with blood. It is now displayed on a mirror held by two silver angels at the tomb of St. John of Nepomuk in the Cathedral.

Bridge, statues, many stories, many battles...but all a part of eternity. I imagine it as the bridge standing over the waters.

<u>CHURCH OF SAINT JOHN OF NEPOMUK/KOSTEL SV. JANA NEPOMUCKEHO</u>
This single-nave Baroque church *(left and p.21)* was built in 1720–1729 by K. I. Dientzenhofer and boasts vault frescoes by V.V. Reiner (1728). Upon its completion, the church was dedicated to St. John of Nepomuk in 1729, the year of his canonization. Originally, the church was owned by the Ursuline convent before the order was ended during the late 18th century reign of Emperor Joseph II, who felt that monasteries belonged to medieval life and should not be a part of the Age of Enlightenment.

OLD TOWN

In the years when I still had some free time and tourists were not yet coming to Prague, I spent hours, or sometimes entire afternoons, in a small pub at the corner of Old Town Square with the old artist Zdenek Bouse, who disliked art and who had been, for the past ten years, reading only one book—Tao te Ting. Other artists and poets were coming, poor, wine-loving, cheerfully sad people, a little bit damned but beautiful. Zdenek told me, "If you will sit here with me for another few years, you may start to understand this place. If this square is the center of Prague and Prague is the center of Europe, are we not drinking in the center of Europe?"

OLD TOWN HALL/STAROMESTKÁ RADNICE
The Old Town Hall was established in 1338 by King John of Luxembourg. As the Old Town Hall quarters grew, the adjoining houses became part of its expansion. The northern Neo-Gothic addition, built in 1838–1848, was destroyed in the last days of World War II. In addition to the row of town-houses, the Old Town Hall includes a tower (1364) and the stained-glass bay window of the Oriel Chapel (1381). The Orloj, or astronomic clock, was acquired in 1410 and is built into the first story of the clock tower building. The clock shows the paths of both the sun and moon across the zodiac, which reflects the belief that Earth was the center of the universe. A calendar below the clock painted by Josef Mánes shows each month and its respective Zodiac sign.

Old Town or Stare Mesto was completed in 1230 when seven original parishes were enclosed by a Romanesque city wall. Old Town comprises some 20 historic churches, more than 700 priceless buildings including 30 palaces and 4 town halls, innumerable works of art and a large helping of mystery. The center of Old Town is the Church of Our Lady Before Týn at Old Town Square (Staroméstské námestí). (The rather enigmatic word *Týn* has the same origin as the Celtic *Duin* or English *town*, meaning a closed space protected by walls.) Old Town is like any other town: a jigsaw puzzle. At some moment, a whole picture will emerge from a number of individual pieces. Most characteristic of the Old Town are its square, Celetná Street, the mighty organs of St. James Church, the tranquil corners of St. Agnes monastery, and the fruit and vegetable stalls of Havel Market.

Where should we go ourselves? The astronomic clocks at Town Hall, constructed around 1410 by Master Mikulás from Kadan, immediately capture our attention. The first thing we realize is that we cannot tell from one clock what time it is—two other clocks are required for orientation. If a modern literate scholar is challenged by the clocks, what about a medieval person? What was the purpose of the clocks? Until the 16th century, clocks were designed by architects and, besides their practical applications, the clocks represented a model of the world composed of gears exactly fitting to each other as in an ideal machine. One of God's nicknames was the Great Watchmaker. Astronomic clocks display the position of Earth, moon and sun, the day of the year, the zodiac sign, and the hours of the day expressed in terms of twenty-four hours (not

twelve hours as on more modern clocks). A Disneyland of wooden apostles parade through two openings near a noisy wooden rooster, Death shaking his head, and several other figures.

The clocks in fact display the state of the universe and serve as a system of early warning for when time will end and the apocalypse will begin. The clocks as a small universe are somehow related to the larger universe, and because both are built according to the same principles, the small universe will be put to a stop before the world ends. It may give enough notice for people to pray for the prolongation of their times.

The situation with the moon, sun and planets is more complex, and a number of hypotheses can be drawn. Let's imagine that for medieval humans, there existed a quite modern concept of synchronicity—the world is changing as a

whole because its parts are mutually interrelated, but change is pursuing its own way in individual parts of the Earth system. The position of heavenly bodies can inform us about the background or basic change from which the secondary changes—like our fate—can be deduced.

Let's take an individual: at birth, the soul is standing naked in front of the face of God. There the soul is given a task and sent to descend to Earth through the spheres of seven planets. At each sphere it will receive clothing of its own, the qualities of the clothes being determined by the positions of the stars when the soul was breathed into its body. Each layer of clothing has some function—it protects or makes vulnerable your emotions, skills or body. We call it astronomy or astrology now, according to whether a scientific or divination principle prevails, but for archaic people, the stars were a means of understanding the world. And even more, because we are partly made of stars, then stars revealed our actual position in this fluid world.

FROM YOUNG FRANZ KAFKA TO GREEN MAN

From in front of the Town Hall we can have a closer look at the decoration of the portal and windows of a nearby Renaissance house, U Minuty. Imagine that you are a young boy named Franz Kafka. He was born just around the corner, his father had a shop at the nearby palace of Golz-Kinsky, and

CHURCH OF OUR LADY BEFORE TÝN/
KOSTEL PANNY MARIE PRED TÝNAM
The Gothic Týn Church was begun in the mid-14th century and completed in the early 1500s. Its magnificent steeples make it one of Old Town's most recognized landmarks. The building houses many original Gothic artifacts and contains the tomb of Danish court astronomer Tycho Brahe (1546–1601). From the early 1400s until 1620, Týn Church was the central Hussite church in Prague. The church is separated from Old Town Square by Týn School, which has one of Prague's oldest Gothic arcades.

"AT THE STONE BELL"/U KAMENNÉHO ZVONU
Old Town Square is lined by many houses and palaces that represent Prague's history and architecture since the Middle Ages. At the Stone Bell is a magnificent, well-preserved 14th-century Gothic town palace, restored in 1980–1987 as a gallery. Its rarity and architectural integrity make At the Stone Bell one of Prague's most important Gothic houses. Also on Old Town Square stands the house At the White Unicorn, birthplace of Czech singer Josefina Dusková, a close friend of Mozart. (p.49)

JAN HUS MONUMENT/POMNÍK JANA HUSA
In the midst of Old Town Square stands the famous Jan Hus statue and monument. It was designed in 1915 by Ladislav Saloun to memorialize the life and deeds of the Czech religious reformer, martyr and University Master Jan Hus. His heroic death (July 6, 1415) in flames of inquisition is commemorated as a Czech national holiday.

**BETHLEHEM CHAPEL/
BETLÉMSKÁ KAPLE**

The reconstructed Bethlehem Chapel *(left)* is a National Cultural Monument. The original chapel, where sermons were preached in Czech instead of the usual Latin, was built on this site in 1394. Between 1402 and 1413, Master Jan Hus delivered sermons here, effectively using the pulpit as a kind of medieval mass medium with the reach of today's newspapers. More than a thousand people could gather in the chapel and several hundred sermons were delivered there during a time when the total population of Prague was less than 40 thousand people.

HAVEL MARKET *(right)*

Franz later worked for years in the house U Minuty. He lived most of his life in Old Town Square, and his apartment had just one window, and it opened into the nave of Týn Church! Consider how deeply the picture books of your childhood are imprinted in your mind; you can recall knights, princesses, dragons, Cinderella, dwarfs and other characters. Kafka did not have many picture books, but he was a close observer of his immediate environment. Around Town Hall, his view included images of a naked woman on a Renaissance house pouring milk from her breasts (allegory of the Earth nurturing humanity), knights in battle, a king hanging from the window of Town Hall, strange animals, a head consuming another head at the 17th-century wooden doors of Town Hall, a distraught Late Gothic face with a pillar in its mouth, a stone owl in a cavern below the astronomic clocks, a hedgehog, a bat, and a basilisk in a circle around the clock's face. It is apparent that the strange symbolism of Kafka's novels is rooted in the fantastic landscape of his childhood. It comes from the spirit of the city.

From the same vantage point, look carefully at Týn church. The right tower is wider than the left one. The southern tower is called Adam, and the slim northern tower is called Eve. During the hot summer day, Adam provides shade for Eve. They are a yin-yang couple, sanctified and linked together by the nave of church to form a unit.

Now proceed to the Gothic arcades of Týn School as we change the topic to medieval biology. At the northern part of the arcades, at the crossing of the ribbed vault, you will see the face of a man encircled by oak leaves. The branches emerging from his mouth tell you that leaves are the words of Green Man. His face can also be found at the bay window of Carolinum just across from the Estate Theater. We know the figure of Green George or Jack-In-the-Green from English or Slavic folklore. During medieval springtime festivals, a man clothed in branches and green leaves was guided through the fields to ensure their fertility. The stone mask of Green Man appears in hidden corners of Romanesque and, more commonly, Gothic architecture. Green Man can be found inside churches, which indicates that he belongs to the sphere of the sacred. The forest is more than a collection of trees; a unifying spirit of soil bacteria, fungi, ants, roots, plants and memory seems to be present. This green, whispering light is Green Man.

THE LANGUAGE OF ARCHITECTURE

Architecture combines practical, utilitarian aspects and noble, spiritual or symbolic meanings. It represents not only the soul of the given epoch but its body as well. Both are expressed as a specific language of forms and spaces, as a "hardware" of buildings and a "software" of ideas. Architecture is a text that can be read or interpreted. One can walk through the historical town as a virtual reality. Fine art is more intellectual, but architecture tells a story of everyday life—how many toilets did the palace have (one on each floor for the average building); when were sewage and water conduits developed. Architecture is a language whose words and sentences can be touched with your hands.

ESTATES THEATRE/STAVOVSKÉ DIVADLO

The Estates Theater (*above*), a National Cultural Monument, was commissioned by Count Nostitz and built in 1783 in the Neoclassical style. Mozart's opera *Don Giovanni* was premiered here on October 29, 1787, as was the 1834 play Fidlovacka, from which the Czech National Anthem ("Where is my Home") was chosen. After numerous renovations and a recent restoration, the Estates Theater was reopened in 1991. The magnificent theater has been an artistic mecca and architectural treasure for visitors and for Czech citizens for more than two hundred years.

CHURCH OF SAINT JOHN ON THE ROCK/KOSTEL SV. JANA NA SKALCE

Built in 1730-1739, the church of St. John on the Rock (*right*) was designed by Kilian Ignaz Dientzenhofer in the Bohemian Baroque style. Its small size coupled with an octagonal floor plan make this one of K. Dientzenhofer's most unique designs; the double towers extend high above the narrow facade, adding to its dramatic scale. The church's altar displays a wooden statue of St. John of Nepomuk, modeled after Jan Brokof's original statue on the Charles Bridge.

MILESTONES OF JEWISH HISTORY IN BOHEMIA:

903-906: Bohemian Jews are for the first time mentioned in a customs document

965: a Jewish merchant from Near East, Ibrahim ibn Jakub, writes the first description of Prague as a town built of stone and mortar (he refers to several churches)

1254: King Premysl Otokar II issues a decree concerning the protection of Jews and religious tolerance; acts of violence and pogroms still occur every few decades

14-16th centuries: Royal privileges and violence alternate, pogroms and attacks are organized but the economy is dependent on Jewish bankers and merchants and needs to be protected

1609: Rabbi Löw, creator of Golem and cabalistic scholar, dies

1648: Jews together with students and inhabitants of Old and New Town win the last battle of the Thirty Years War against the Swedish army attacking across Charles Bridge from Mala Strana

18th century: Fires occur in Prague, and blame falls on the Jews. They are expelled from the city center during the reign of Empress Maria Theresa, but they soon return when Emperor Joseph II, a subscriber to the precepts of the Enlightenment, partially suspends the anti-Jewish policy.

19th century: a gradual rise of the Jewish bourgeoisie and banking sector

1939-1945: 77,297 Jews die in concentration camps

JEWISH QUARTER/JOSEFOV

The historical record mentions the founding of the first Jewish community in Prague at around 1091. During the Middle Ages, the city had two separate settlements; Western Jews lived near the Old-New Synagogue, and Byzantine Jews chose to settle near the site of the Spanish Synagogue. Over the years the two communities combined and formed an enclosed ghetto. In Prague, as in many cities where they settled, Jews were alternately respected and discriminated against. Emperor Joseph II's initiation of reforms toward Prague's Jews was acknowledged in the Jewish Quarter's being renamed as Josefov. This area of Old Town was formally granted independent status as a district of Prague in 1850. The extremely old ghetto buildings had suffered during the violent pogroms, and many had to be demolished in the late 18th century due to sanitation problems. However, the monuments that still remain house the largest collection of sacred Jewish artifacts in the world.

JEWISH CEMETERY

The Jewish Cemetery was founded in the early 15th century and is now part of the State Jewish Museum. It has more than 12,000 Late Gothic, Renaissance and Baroque-era tombs, including the precious tomb of Renaissance thinker Rabbi Löw (c.1520–1609), who, according to legend, created the Golem, an artificial man. This site was for more than three hundred years the only burial ground available to Jews in Prague. Inside the old Pinkas Synagogue is a memorial bearing the names of 77,000 Czech Jews who died in the Holocaust.

JEWISH TOWN

Some of the most important things about Prague I have learned not in books but from oral tradition. A lady once turned to me at Old-New Synagogue, asking: "Do you know why this synagogue was never destroyed? There is an angel flying above it holding an invisible protective veil." I immediately felt the truth in her statement, because I had often had the feeling of something unique, maybe a light pyramid, above this place. This angel must be different from all other angels, a cabalistic one composed of letters of the Hebraic alphabet. You cannot communicate with him in ordinary non-mathematical language.

The Jewish memorials in Prague are considered to be among the most precious Jewish monuments of Europe. The earliest Jewish settlements were scattered in Mala Strana, below Vysehrad, and in New Town south of the Narodni metro station where a Jewish cemetery from 1270 was discovered during recent construction work.

The Jewish town of Josefov is located approximately in the middle of Old Town close to the Vltava river. The Old Jewish Cemetery (established in 1439, containing at least twelve thousand headstones), six synagogues and an extremely rich Jewish museum are the most significant memorials in Josefov, but for sitting in quiet contemplation over the touching and mournful fate of the local Jewish community, I suggest a visit to the forlorn New Jewish Cemetery where Franz Kafka's grave is located (at Zelivského metro station), or to the almost neglected historical Jewish cemetery under the Zizkov TV tower. Several other synagogues, mostly simple and modern (from 1890–1920), were built in other parts of Prague —near Palmovka metro station, you will find a grey synagogue that hosts concertos and art performances.

Prague's Jewish ghetto, a pitiful, unhealthy maze of poor, dirty houses, was destroyed more than a century ago. If you want to imagine and maybe understand its life, you should visit the Moravian town of Trebíc, where the whole Jewish quarter (including two synagogues and a large cemetery) is preserved. I believe that without seeing Trebíc, one cannot comprehend Prague's Jewish town; one cannot imagine Golem walking its streets.

In the Middle Ages, Prague represented the eastern gateway for Jews coming primarily from eastern and southern Europe over the Russian steppes and along the Danube. The western gateways from the Middle East through northern Africa were Toledo and other Spanish towns. From the 16th to the 18th century, Christian culture was strongly influenced by Jewish philosophy, alchemy and cabala, an occult philosophy based on a mystical interpretation of the scriptures. By the 19th century, Prague was a town comprising Czech, German and Jewish cultures. A nomadic, well-educated intellectual elite of Jewish origin, including architects and artists, connected and homogenized central Europe.

It is difficult to be poetic when talking about Jewish Town's history, because the specter of the Holocaust hangs like a veil between us and the pre-Holocaust history. It is difficult to comprehend the role of Jews in diverse revolutionary and reformation movements (e.g., there were many ethnic Jews among Jesuits). People often tend to look at Prague's history from 1848–1938 from the perspective of three ethnic groups alternately cooperating and fighting with each other. In fact, however, grave conflicts existed within each group—atheists and socialists or Catholics and Protestants among Czechs; Germans of Austrian and of Prussian orientation; the rich, godless Jewish technocracy and poor religious Jews influenced by Hasidism (a sect of Jewish mystics that originated in Poland and Russia). For me, the most touching element of old central European Jewish ghettos is the image of a unruly pub at the lower floor of a building, while up in the attic a man sits studying, praying and talking to God. Demons at street level, angels in the upper floor.

PRIMEVAL GOLEM

The origin of the legend of Golem is based on the mystical Hebraic teachings and writings of the cabala. According to the tradition, stones have one soul, animals and plants have two souls but man has three souls. The two lower souls can be created, but the third soul, which is a part of God, can be breathed in only by Jehovah. The holy books like Sefer Jecira or Bereshit contain seven texts. The first text is written in letters and printed; all the other texts are like onion layers hidden invisibly in the spaces between the lines. But how can

OLD-NEW SYNAGOGUE/
STARONOVÁ SYNAGOGA

Prague's Old-New Synagogue (originally called New Synagogue), built c.1270 in the Early Gothic style, is one of Europe's oldest surviving synagogues. Although it has withstood fire and attack and undergone partial reconstruction, the distinctive building retains its 13th century appearance. Inside the single-nave sanctuary, two large pillars support the massive five-rib vaulting. The synagogue has been a sacred place of refuge for over seven centuries and is still the religious center of Jewish life in Prague. Preserved relics include a chair often used by 16th century thinker Rabbi Löw and the Ark Shrine that holds scrolls of the holy Torah.

JEWISH TOWN HALL/
ZIDOVSKÁ RADNICE

Across from the Old-New Synagogue in Jewish Town stands the beautiful Jewish Town Hall. The original core of the structure was built in 1577 by Pancratius Roder in the Renaissance style. Commissioned by the wealthy mayor Mordechai Maisel, the town hall has served Prague's Jewish district of Old Town since its founding under Hapsburg Emperor Joseph II. Alterations in the Rococco style in 1763 were by Josef Schlesinger, and its 20th century expansion added the southern wing. The building's tower has a clock with Roman numerals, and its 3rd story pediment holds a second clock that features Hebrew numerals and runs counterclockwise. The Jewish Town Hall now houses the Council of Jewish Religious Communities in the Czech Republic.

you be certain that your understanding of the different layers of invisible text is complete? You must perform an experiment of creating two lower souls and implementing them into a body of clay. It is a golem. The word means imperfect, unfinished, primeval. Golem is a raw material that must be developed. To make a golem was a kind of a final exam—matter does not lie. If you were able to create a golem, your understanding of one layer of the text was complete and you could proceed further.

Rabbi Löw's Golem was an artificial man, created from the four natural elements, to protect the community. But the Golem went on a rampage one evening and his spark of life had to be removed. Mary Shelley used the concept of an artificial being in her novel Frankenstein, and since then it has been revived as innumerable robots and terminators. The problem is always the same: how to create a mind that will not demolish objects and ruin relationships, because humankind has always the constructive soul and destructive shadow.

CABALA

A friend of mine worked for more than ten years translating a short text from Sefer Jecira into Czech. This Hebraic text has a mathematical meaning, because each letter corresponds to a certain number, and the sum of the letters makes a mathematical sequence. The book is an evolving mathematical progression, and the translation should thus respect the accuracy of the written text and the underlying mathematical principles.

Similar principles are used in the symbolic art of Christian cabala, especially from the Baroque period. A symbol of a crucified snake appears at several Baroque monasteries (Plasy, Kladruby, Broumov). Aside from the visual and textual symbolism of the crucified snake as Jesus Christ, there is a mathematical symbolism—the sum of the letters of the Hebraic expression for copper snake is the same as for Messiah.

FAVORITE PARKS AND GARDENS

PETRÍN HILL/PETRÍNSKÉ SADY

Petrín Hill is a place of many attractions. The century-old Observation Tower, a small replica of the Eiffel Tower, was built in 1891 for the Jubilee Exhibition. A labyrinth named the "Mirror Maze", built in 1891, contains a diorama of the famous 1648 battle, "The Defense of Prague against the Swedes." An ancient church (the Church of Saint Laurence, above left) was built on Petrín Hill in the 10th century by Prince Boleslav II to cover a pagan site. The original building was of a Romanesque style, and was later rebuilt with a Baroque exterior in the 1700s. On lower Petrín Hill is the Kinsky Villa, which houses the Czech National Museum's Ethnographic Exposition (Folklore Museum). On its grounds stands a small church built in the 18th century and transported here in 1929 as a gift from Slovakians in the newly-acquired Czech territory, Ruthenia, bordering Ukraine. Petrín Hill's Park is a blossoming garden orchard covered with winding paths leading to the summit, which commands sweeping views over Mala Strana, Old Town, and Hradcany. The 300-year old orchards were planted over 12th-century vineyards, which grew where an ancient forest blanketed the hill and stretched 4 miles all the way to White Mountain (Bílá Hora) west of the city.

FRANCISCAN GARDEN/FRANTISKÁNSKÁ ZAHRADA

Near Wenceslas Square in New Town is the Franciscan garden (above), an old monastery garden that now serves as a park. In the middle of a bustling area, the peaceful park (opened to the public in 1950) has recently begun growing herbs and other plants similar to those grown by the Franciscan monks who used to live here.

LETNA PARK/LETENSKÉ SADY

Letna Park (top right) is situated on a plateau just outside the city, across the river from Jewish Town. In medieval times, enemy armies gathered here to attack the city's stronghold at Prague Castle. Letna has been parkland since the 1850s and is now a public park. The Hanavsky Pavilion was moved here after the 1891 Jubilee Exhibition. Its Neo-Baroque architecture, formed with contemporary materials—glass and iron—shows the humble beginnings of modern high-rise buildings.

THREE KINDS OF LOVE

Love has many countenances, but it is one and in fact indivisible. Sometimes love arises as a natural magnetism, but at other times there is a conscious decision and will to love. Medieval theology distinguished three basic types of love that grow in ever-widening circles from the individual to the family and then to the community and beyond. The first stage is often called eros, a kind of love where both body and mind are involved in a certain balance. It evolves through the cultivation of sexual desires and often is depicted in scenes from the garden of pleasures. The next stage may be called filia and is a love for your children, for friends and others. Filia develops into agape, a widening embrace of the whole community, country, nature and cosmos. Love does not simply happen; it should be cultivated like a field.

GARDENS OF DELIGHT AND COUNTENANCE

Gardening is an opportunity to return to lost Paradise. Most European gardens combine aspects of three basic types of gardens: The Italian garden is small and geometric (in contrast to nature), with walls, statues, and fountains. The French garden displays grandeur and a well-defined axis; stone walls are replaced by shrubs pruned into architecture. The English garden is as picturesque as a Gainsborough etching and blends into the forest, where you can hunt for a fox.

Prague's largest park is Stromovka, a former royal hunting ground with a medieval castle that was later rebuilt in Neo-Gothic style. Still visible is the island with old oak trees, where Emperor Rudolf II once organized his banquets and symposiums with philosophers and artists. In the mornings, he would board a ship to the nearby Emperor's mill, where Italian jewelers taught him how to cut and polish precious gemstones. Nearby in the Exhibition Grounds, the Lapidarium beautifully displays statues and archaeological remnants dating back to Gothic times.

Petrín is a park for lovers and a place to encounter stunning vistas of Prague. On the high side of the park runs the Hunger Wall, so named because Charles IV ordered the project to provide employment for poor residents.

Wallenstein Garden, entered just behind the Malostranská Metro station, has peacocks on the meadow and fish in the pond, a grotto, elegant bronze statues—it might be the best moment of a hot July day.

The South Gardens step down toward Malá Strana from the castle. Two obelisks mark the spot where two Imperial Catholic governors were thrown by Protestant nobles from an upper palace window to protest the intolerant Hapsburg Archduke Ferdinand's succession to the throne. This famous 1618 Defenestration of Prague marked the beginning of the Thirty Years War.

The Royal Gardens offer breathtaking views of the cathedral and lead to one of the most beauteous Renaissance buildings north of the Alps: the Belvedere or Royal Summer Palace of Queen Anne. In front of the Belvedere, you can sit under the bronze bell-like bowl of the Singing Fountain and listen to the musical rhythm of the water drops. A marvelous experience!

ROYAL SUMMER PALACE/KRALOVSKY LETOHRADEK

This Renaissance building known also as Belvedere was begun in 1538 by architect Paolo della Stella. Situated in front of the palace is the famous Singing Fountain, built during the 16th century by bellmaker Tomás Jaros. The fountain was engineered so exquisitely that as water falls on the bronze basin, its ringing sound sings on through the centuries. The surrounding gardens offer some of the most beautiful views of the Castle.

IN PRAISE OF PERIPHERY

In outlying areas of the city lie treasures less discovered and unchanged through centuries.

BENEDICTINE ABBEY OF ST. MARGARET

The monastery was built in a marsh on oak piles, which perhaps were intended to cork the spring to prevent demons from passing into our world. The medieval conception of the devil as something of a conniving terrorist led Benedictine monks to hold constant prayer guard.

The second most important Baroque monument of Prague *(right)* was built at the sacred spring called Vojteska. According to legend, in 993, a knight chasing elk encountered St. Adalbert (Vojtech) and vowed to the saint to build here Bohemia's second monastery (the first was St. George at the Castle).

Baroque architects Christoph and Kilian Ignaz Dientzenhofer delicately preserved the pre-Romanesque crypt located under the church while adding colorful frescoes depicting the life and miracles of St. Benedict, St. Adalbert, and St. Gunther (Vintír) as well as the generously undulating walls of the Baroque masterpiece. Far from being a fossilized monument whose active life has ended, this functioning monastery continues its history into the present and future.

SYMBOL OF ETERNITY

I recently took my students to a medieval monastery in central Bohemia. The place was three times burnt down, eleven times robbed, several times abandoned, and twice the monks were killed. It was shut down by Maria Theresa and again later by the Communist regime. Imagine the destruction of the World Trade Center, repeated over centuries. Now the monks are again returning to the monastery.

During the Middle Ages, a peacock feather was the symbol of eternity. At first glance, a feather would seem less durable than steel and concrete. But a feather is flexible and renews itself every year. Eternity is the urge and the capacity to continue and, like the peacock feather, it contains an element of beauty.

CHURCH OF ST. WENCESLAS

This church serves local people who recharge the place with their esteem and devotion.

St. Wenceslas, the "Good King Wenceslas" of the Christmas Carol, encouraged missionaries to come to Bohemia from Germany and founded the Rotunda of St. Vitus at the current site of the cathedral. He was murdered by his pagan brother Boleslav and became Bohemia's patron saint. The Romanesque church of St. Wenceslas *(left)* was founded in Prosek after 929 at the site where the procession transporting the martyred king's body* to Prague stopped for a rest. The simple interior of the church displays some peculiar features; the columns are decorated by rough engravings of two pillars (possibly Jakin and Boas from Solomon's temple), a lily, and seeds of life resembling beans. At the apse of the right nave, the wall is covered with red swastikas (possibly from the end of the 13th century), often used as a symbol of the sun in ancient cultures. The gentle mystery of the church connects you to the life of a 19th-century village and, because people in pre-industrial times preserved traditions, you may have a glimpse of centuries past. *(*p.20)*

48

VILLA BERTRAMKA

Mozart stayed several times at Bertramka, composing, among other pieces, Don Giovanni *behind a stone table located at the upper part of villa garden. He was perhaps in love with Josefina and he composed for her an aria, "Goodbye my Beautiful Flame", but history is in this case so decent that it closes its objective eyes before the subjective histories of mortals.*
But music remains.

Villa Bertramka was a vineyard house bought for celebrated opera singer Josefina Duskova in 1784. She married an older man, Frantisek Dusek, a composer and pianist who in his day was a key musical figure of Prague. Dusek taught Czech composer Leopold Kozeluh, who succeeded Wolfgang Amadeus Mozart in the position of court composer. Dusek, who lived for some time in Salzburg, knew Mozart's family well. As Josefina's grandfather was mayor of Salzburg, she participated in the town's social life.

The Duseks regularly exchanged letters with Mozart, following Mozart's rise and his struggles with the Italian musical mafia. (Händel faced the same problems in London, and Dvorák had to deal with the legacy of Italian music in New York). Italians at European courts were organized almost as a musical monopoly and, for German, Czech or Austrian musicians and

W. A. MOZART MUSEUM/BERTRAMKA

Originally a 17th-century homestead farmhouse, Bertramka was converted into a large country villa by Frantisek and Josefina Dusek in the late 18th century. Mozart's opera Don Giovanni was composed here especially for the city of Prague. Bertramka now houses an extensive Mozart exhibit devoted to his life, work and legacy.

composers, they were an almost impermeable barrier. Central Europe's musical feeling is, compared to the Italian, less sweet, more austere, often with traces of humor and even sarcasm.

The Mannheim school, and others where many Czech composers participated, laid the groundwork for the music of Mozart. We often tend to view history as the acts of a few extraordinary persons, but such personalities are in fact encircled by other artists—Germans call them "Kleinemeister," or small masters. They are not as distinguished as the great masters, but they produce some artistic treasures and often reveal and elaborate on other aspects of music. Czech small masters associated with Mozart's music were, besides Dusek, Josef Myslivecek, J. V. Stamic and J. A. Benda.

Mozart understood their art, and his genius elevated this older musical strain to new heights. Prague loved Mozart in return. Prague was the first town to pay tribute to the premature death of Mozart in a great, solemn requiem mass celebrated for his soul and performed by 120 musicians in the church of St. Nicholas in 1791.

TROY CHATEAU

The axis of the chateau as seen from the center of the staircase points to Prague Castle to express the politically correct attitudes of the local aristocrat—but his loyalty is somehow conditional; the axis does not intersect the royal office but the Church of All Saints.

TROJA PALACE/TROJSKY ZAMEK

Troja Palace was designed for Count Sternberg by Jean-Baptiste Mathey in the classical Italian villa style in the late 17th century. The palace complex is embraced by Bohemia's first Baroque French-style gardens. Some of the palace's most important features are the Garden Staircase (a grand oval entrance leading to the front entry), the Grand Hall frescoes by Abraham Goydn, and the Formal Gardens with its network of statuary, paths and terraces.

Like many chateaux, Troy has gardens more splendid than its interior. But as you walk up the monumental staircase, be prepared for terrifying theater. Above the main entrance, we see Virtue extinguishing the fire of a torch over the trunk of a demon of war. Lamb and lion are peacefully resting under her feet. The monumental staircase is encircled by statues of ancient gods and goddesses, but there is in the center a disturbing abyss in which two angry giants are lying under a stone thrown onto their bellies. The scene depicts the Greek Gigants who were summoned by the goddess Gaia to revolt against the Olympian gods. What is the meaning of this scene, and why after millennia is it repeated here?

The chateau was built between the Thirty Years War (1618–1648) and the Turkish wars (which continued for centuries). Imagine the vast armies of the Thirty Years War marching through Europe, often hungry and without any logistic support. Up to 40,000 soldiers could be accompanied by 3–5 times that many servants, craftsmen and even wives and children. These 200,000 angry, ruthless people without perspective were seeking not the enemy but their withheld salary and some basic security. At times they did not fight, but they were constantly seeking food. Small companies of soldiers were sent out to steal food from local farmers, who were then left to starve. Entire villages of people hid in the forests with their cattle or ran into remote sandstone canyons to hide. Typical of the situation were tortures, rapes, sufferings of all kinds. Swedish King Gustavus Adolphus' threat of total war meant that every village was burned down, their apple trees cut, their wells poisoned by carcasses. No other army could follow in the steps of this terrible death squadron, which left more than a ten-mile-wide swath of burnt land and dying people behind. Armies were thus for thirty years making complex maneuvers in central Europe. Diplomatic missions were more common than battles, because more could be achieved through them. Almost everybody who perished in that war died from of disease and hunger.

Thrown into the abyss at the monumental staircase of Troy are not some abstract Greek gods, but the dark forces of irrational chaos in which people's lives have no meaning.

HVEZDA (STAR) CHATEAU

*The six-pointed star usually means in symbolic
language the balance between duties to God
(a triangle pointing up) and to family and Earth
(a triangle pointing down). In Marian liturgy, one of the
images of Our Lady is the marine star—a star shining
and leading a ship on a sea that is so violent that you
cannot tell where the sea ends and the sky begins.*

When French surrealist André Breton visited star-shaped Hvezda, a poem about a chateau standing at the edge of a chasm, a chateau made of the Philosopher's Stone, came to his lips. He was so haunted by stars that there is one engraved on his tombstone.

A star is a kind of beacon, one you need when lost or confused. Archduke Ferdinand of Tyrol had this star-shaped chateau built according his own plan as a place of solace and consolation (1555). He was caught in a dilemma, one of his own choosing: He secretly married a rich merchant's daughter, Filipina Welser, who was of lowly origin, and therefore he could not become the royal successor. Also, he faced uncertain times of war and religious reformation; in the entire century there were scarcely three years devoid of major European conflict. He needed the star of guidance and spiritual strength.

In the center of Hvezda's main hall we see among the delicate, highly detailed stucco work the hero Aeneas, who leaves burning Troy (which was destroyed for the love of a woman). A star appears above him that leads him to Italy to establish a new, powerful empire—Rome. What a dream for the Archduke! The main axis of the chateau leads through a corridor dedicated to a stucco goddess Venus in the central position of the vault, to a window through which the actual star Venus appears. From this perspective, we see the star as the spiritual beacon of Our Lady, a star as the love for which the Archduke sacrificed the royal throne, a star leading Aeneas to establish a new empire, and a real astronomical star appearing as the governing principle of the chateau's orientation.

Maybe one day I shall be allowed to tell how this remarkable chateau still quiets the hearts of confused lovers. I often observe that historical buildings seem to function according to a software imposed in them centuries ago.

LIVING AMONG IMPS AND POLITICAL ECONOMY

I observe the bears in Ceský Krumlov's castle moat. They are apple-eating bears, retired from the circus. It is a clear early morning; the courtyard is totally abandoned. They play in their swimming pool like children, pushing an empty aluminum beer barrel under the surface and propelling it out of the water. Then they play water polo with an old stump. My brown brothers, *I tell them,* you are human when no one is watching, but when people come, you disguise yourselves as animals. *I sit at the bench, aware of another consciousness of walls, waters and geology. I realize that we can plan a comfortable town for ourselves that excludes gods, demons and imps. But to whom will our soul then talk in the dark abyss of despair or in luminous awareness?*

Contrary to the popular belief that towns gradually coalesced from villages, most central European towns were established between 1220–1280, and most were established in one day. We can distinguish three types of towns, as follows:

Antique towns originated as early as four thousand years ago and more. Some of them survived the fall of the Roman empire as mere shadows of their former glory, such as Paris, Geneva and towns along the Donau (Danube) River. However, towns in Byzantine areas were stable until the 15th century. European crusaders were often shocked to find, in seemingly barbarian regions, advanced towns with perfect sewage systems, water conduits and enlightened citizens.

Evolved towns gradually developed (mostly since the 8th–10th centuries) near significant castles and government centers, and close to fords and marketplaces. These towns are usually labyrinthine, with a narrow and irregular central square.

Planned towns are the most common in Central Europe. In many cases, they were established on a green meadow near existing evolved cities where there was room for a large market square. This is the case in Ceský Krumlov, where a narrow evolved town is located directly under the castle, and the planned or New Town was established across the river. Ceské Budejovice is an excellent example of a centrally planned town with a rectangular network of street lines. Planned towns often have a large, square central area, with two perpendicular axes that extend from the square, dividing the town into four quarters.

Most planned towns were established by whoever was king at the time. During the 13th century, kings throughout Europe were losing status because the aristocracy were dividing the land into dominions (areas resembling small kingdoms) under their own exclusive control. Armies had grown larger, and towns were superseding castles in importance. But even in such a divided land, the king could still control the country with the help of royal towns, which could serve as economic and military fortresses.

Construction of a town was administered by a locator. He chose a place—usually on a major merchant route or, even better, at the intersection of two roads some thirteen to twenty miles, or one day's travel, from the next town. He called in rich people who, as burghers, were guaranteed a set of privileges: personal freedom; a twelve-year suspension of all taxes; the right to operate a market, brew beer, quarry stone and participate in major regional decisions. In return, each burgher was required to build a stone house (using stone helped to prevent city fires) bordering the square. During the 14th century, most towns prospered and grew. Within a few decades of the town foundation, city walls were built and a town hall established.

THE CIVIL SOCIETY

In order to understand the common base of European civilization, we should be aware of its roots. They are three: Christianity, urban culture and the market economy. The last two are closely interwoven with mining, education and town growth.

During the 13th century, one of the defining moments of European life occurred: the transition from the barter system to the widespread use of currency. The tax systems underwent a drastic change, with taxes being collected no longer as harvest but in monetary form. The change of the monetary and tax system was a crucial step that triggered many other changes. Mining, silver production and mints were now required, and by the year 1250, several million small, silver coins were already in circulation. And if tax collectors wanted to collect money instead of crops, they had to keep records and create the optimal conditions for marketplace development and market freedoms.

While life in a village continues as ever in a cycle of harvests and winters, a town's progress is linear, never fully returning to its origins. The early Middle Ages were characterized by competition between clergy and aristocracy, but the emergence of burghers during the 13th–14th century was followed in the 15th century by mighty guilds representing the trades. The new class of active, independent burghers of low origin and high ambitions began to trigger vast changes. Their support for centers of education other than monasteries gave rise to universities

that developed into nearly independent sources of ideas.

Without towns, there would not be a modern civil society. Economic freedoms open the door to civil and, later, human rights. It is difficult to establish a civil society in the absence of the complex market freedoms that lay the groundwork for democracy.

The progress of the town in central Europe followed a certain pattern. Typically, a town was established in the 13th century, underwent rapid development, then was partly destroyed in the Hussite wars of the 1420s. During the Renaissance, it gradually recovered its noble houses and often doubled its former size, then was destroyed again during the Thirty Years War (1618–1648). For the next century, it struggled to regain its former level of living, and then was largely stable until 1840–1860, when intensive industrialization took place. Around 1860, the city walls were removed and the town rapidly expanded along railway lines and major roads. Two percent of the population lived in towns in Gothic times, some three or four percent lived there in Renaissance years, only six percent at the beginning of the 20th century, and now more than half of Europeans live in towns.

Yes, without understanding urban history and its social significance, we will never be able to find an appropriate place for our restless lives. But you keep looking into my eyes, laughingly rejecting the serious science of urbanism, and you ask: Do you really believe that all the dragons of your life were just princesses awaiting deeds of bravery and beauty? Are you unaware that imps have never been seen in a steel and glass building, while they are abundant in this dirty and chaotic corner? *I try to answer:* The flowers and the wind will never justify this arranged tidiness. *After some hesitation I add a verse of the Moravian poet Jan Skácel:* If I shall send away all my demons, all my angels will be gone with them. *And you seem to understand that some of the best things were never planned, that young people need mud.*

TEPLÁ MONASTERY/KLÁSTER TEPLÁ

Teplá Monastery was founded in 1197 about eight miles from one of the healing mineral springs that are numerous in the western region of Bohemia. Over the years, the monks extended the use of the springs to weary travelers, the ailing faithful, and area noblemen by building a pilgrim's lodge and tapping the mineral water into barrels for sale. An enormous library collection at Teplá Monastery has more than 70,000 books and manuscripts, some dating from the 9th century. The building houses a museum filled with priceless Baroque objects, instruments and artwork.

KUTNÁ HORA
…and death shall have no dominion

Kutná Hora was for several centuries the second most important city in the Bohemian kingdom, due to one of the largest silver deposits in Europe and due to the 14th-century mines that reached a depth of 1600 feet. In its time of glory, some three thousand miners produced two to five tons of silver annually. The town is the home of the oldest Bohemian cathedral and is listed as UNESCO World Heritage Site.

INCREDIBLE OSSUARY

The famous Chapel of All Saints with the ossuary and cemetery belongs to the nearby monastery of Sedlec. Founded by a group of Cistercian monks in 1142, the monastery owned properties where silver ore was later discovered, and it thus became one of the richest Bohemian monasteries. You will notice the large, originally Gothic church, which, after destruction by Hussites, was rebuilt in a unique Czech style, an architectonic synthesis of traditional Gothic elements with the dynamic and brighter Baroque style.

The Chapel of All Saints is a charnel, an answer to a dual problem of the lack of urban space and a papal decree stating that human bones must never be found at the Earth's surface. It is a two-story chapel in which the upper floor was dedicated to all saints, and the lower, underground floor stored human bones. This charnel contains the bones of forty thousand people. Four large pyramids of bones were constructed during the Baroque period, and ventilation channels intersected in the center of each pyramid. Gold-plated wooden crowns representing victory over death's dominion were placed over the pyramids.

The numbers of bones continued to increase through the centuries, and woodcarver Frantisek Rint was assigned the task of creating order in their arrangement. He, his wife and two children worked for ten years (until 1872) to produce designs of singular and peculiar beauty: a chandelier containing all the bones of the human body, a coat of arms of the locally prominent Schwarzenberg family arranged in human bones, skulls hanging like a huge rosary from the wall. Was he insane, or did he reflect the late Baroque attitude that everything must be viewed from the point of death, the final judge and door guardian to the afterlife? Love and death were, in those days, much closer than they are today.

The district town of Kutná Hora lies about forty-four miles east of Prague in central Bohemia. During the Middle Ages, the town ranked second in importance and civic beauty after Prague due to its economic, political and cultural wealth, and it was the unrivaled mining center of Bohemia. Its mint produced Prague's widely circulated groschen coins, making the Bohemian king the richest in Europe. The mint building, now called the Valachian Court, was built in 1300 and remodeled for King Wenceslas IV in about 1400 as a temporary royal residence.

The magnificent Bohemian Gothic Church of St. Barbara *(oposite, above)* was built with funds raised by Kutná Hora's miners and was named after their patron saint. Built in 1380, the church boasts three sweeping spires with masses of flying buttresses supporting the tent-shaped vault. The nave contains preserved murals and paintings from the Middle Ages, some of which depict mining scenes and coin production.

SEDLEC OSSUARY/KOSTNICE SEDLEC

The nearby Chapel of All Saints *(opposite, below)* was built in the 14th Century and was damaged by Hussites in the following century. Later rebuilt by in the early Baroque style by Giovanni Santini, the chapel features statues of Saints John of Nepomuk, Václav, Vojtech, Prokop, and Florian lining the entrance to the chapel. The famous Sedlec Ossuary is in the lower floor of the chapel. The interior was ornately decorated by master woodcarver Frantisek Rint in 1870, using more than 40,000 human bones from the adjoining cemetery. The bones, from victims of a 1348 plague epidemic and the 15th-century Hussite wars, were masterfully arranged inside the chapel and on chalices, a monstrance, inscriptions, and coats of arms. The ossuary has a chandelier made with every bone in the human body. The bone decorations, sacred and functional, symbolize the unseen generational connection between human ancestors, the living and their descendants. The number of skulls may represent the multitudes of dead waiting in front of throne of God for resurrection.

A WALK THROUGH KUTNÁ HORA

While the layout of Kutná Hora may seem to reflect the chaotic urbanism of a mining town, recent analysis has determined that the altars of its major churches are exactly 420 meters apart and that its three most important religious festivals occur exactly 111 days apart. As in other medieval towns, a certain invisible order of space and of time underlies the town structure.

Kutná Hora (Mining Mountain) was established where the fertile belt of the Labe valley approaches low, rolling hills. Long houses of Neolithic settlements and Celtic and Slavic fortifications predated the town. The first mint in the area existed more than one thousand years ago.

My language is not noble enough to talk about the magnificent cathedral of St. Barbara. Just stand there under the vault, feel the purified space, and don't miss the huge fresco of St. Cristof, because the day you see him, you will not die! I would need this whole book to explain how architecture and music are related here, how Gregorian chant and Gothic building are different expressions of the same principles. My words are less important than the space around you. The old architecture is written in a universal language that speaks from heart to heart and does not need any syllables.

Walk down to the town along the Jesuit college—a row of statues was erected on the balustrade to resemble Charles Bridge. At the center of Kutná Hora is the large church of St. James (Jakub) and the Valachian Court. The latter is the place where, in 1300, the royal mint reformed by Italian bankers began to coin large, valuable silver pieces called groschen. Before the reform, a number of local currencies existed, so at each market you had to deal with some crooked moneychanger. The monetary reform of late 13th century helped create a new economy established on market freedom.

BIRTH OF THE DOLLAR

During the 16th century, most European silver deposits declined in competition with abundant and cheap Mexican and Bolivian silver. The significant exception was Jáchymov in western Bohemia, located some thirteen miles from Karlovy Vary (Carlsbad) at the foot of forested Krusné hory (Ore Mountains) The silver rush started here in 1516, and within a few years the town became the second most populous after Prague. While the groschen of Kutná Hora represented for a century one of the most widely accepted silver currencies of Europe, the even larger coin produced in Jáchymov soon became the European measure of the standard silver coin. The coin was called Joachimsthaler (literally, a coin from Joachim's valley), but the name was shortened to thaler or tolar. The American silver dollar has the same weight and size as the original Renaissance tolar from the Ore Mountains, and for this reason the recently reconstructed mint of Jáchymov is called the cradle of the American dollar.

SOUTHERN BOHEMIA
WHERE BEAUTY STOPPED WANDERING

In southern Bohemia, an unsurpassed array of towns bearing the seal of the five-petalled rose is scattered like jewels in the landscape. The five-petalled rose is the sign of the Rosenberg family.

TELC

One of the classic ways to comprehend a place is to read a book in the chateau's garden (painting is even better, but not everybody can paint). The book will slowly absorb you and you will forget where you are, but you will open up to the text and, through this openness, the spirit of the place will look with curiosity at you.

Telc is a friendly, nice lady without any side thoughts or provocative secrets. The best way to approach the town is by a pedestrian road paved by heavy granite blocks that will lead you from a rough but charming statue of Our Lady at the former village center, along ponds rimmed by Baroque statues, to the town. Under a linden tree, notice a statue of an uncommon saint—St. Vendelin—who is a patron of shepherds accompanying their herds on the long road from Austria to Moravia. A small limestone sheep looks humbly up at you from behind the saint's feet.

Telc's arms will open suddenly as you enter the long market street. Renaissance and Baroque houses display their colorful gables of many shapes and uniform height. These houses are not competing with each other; they create a common space. Telc's small medieval castle was rebuilt into a large chateau where the ghost of White Lady sometimes will appear, but local people do not talk about such matters to foreigners.

56

RENAISSANCE POLYPHONY

The Renaissance towns of Southern Bohemia are like one town with several centers. They are complementary and one may understand them as a polyphony of voices. The middle ages were musically monophonic, with voices joined in a single melody; Baroque music embraces contrasts in a grandiose concerto. But the Renaissance was polyphonic: a complex musical space was created by climbing and descending choirs, but the whole remained balanced and harmonious.

HISTORIC TELC SQUARE/NÁMESTÍ V TELCI

The town of Telc is in the district of Jihlava in South Moravia. Known as the "Venice of Moravia," Telc was founded in the 13th century as a water fort. A fire in 1530 destroyed some of the town's medieval buildings; however, many remain among the Renaissance-style reconstruction. A continuous arcade connects the square's Renaissance and Baroque townhouses. The entire town of Telc was added to the UNESCO World Cultural and Natural Heritage List in 1993.

CESKÝ KRUMLOV

I remember a morning when I walked through the streets, observing them as if reading a beloved book for the last time. I let myself be drawn into minute fissures in old walls, and there I met the fragments of other fates, pieces of sentences, shadows of loves, and I tried to escape because the place was far too intimate. Then I felt the presence of an ancient woman, Lady of the Spring, and when she came to my mind the water in the courtyard fountain started to flow.

Many consider Ceský Krumlov to be the second most picturesque Bohemian town after Prague. The setting even resembles Prague. Over a steep, rocky ridge above the Vltava River towers the second largest castle in Bohemia. As in Prague, Old Town is situated across the river, and the largest church bears the name of St. Vitus.

Before the Velvet Revolution of 1989 ended Communism, the town was almost deserted. Because of its proximity to the Austrian border, it hosted a military garrison and was otherwise nearly empty. The town was gray, melancholic and, with only a few cheap beer pubs, it was hard to find a meal after 8 PM. In the pubs, townspeople discussed the harsh winter, and Romas, or Gypsies, were sometimes heard singing and dancing behind a campfire in the courtyard of the former monastery.

Now you find the thriving town repaired and painted, the formerly dark, tense buildings glowing with new colors, and a taste of sweet Italy in the red geraniums and in the cheerful faces emerging from bars at midnight. But I am not fooled. In the autumn when it becomes colder and darker, people will retreat into their houses, and you will smell the wood and rocks again. The Vltava, darkened by its peat bogs, will infuse you with strange specters. It is not a town where one would dare to fall in love.

CESKÝ KRUMLOV CASTLE

The glorious Medieval and Renaissance castle, the seat of the south Bohemian aristocratic families, stands above the Vltava River at Ceský Krumlov. Ceský Krumlov was founded in the 13th century. The district town is 108 miles south of Prague and has been described as the Pearl of the Renaissance. The entire area was placed on the UNESCO World Cultural and Natural Heritage List in 1992. Ceský Krumlov Castle and Chateau, originally built in 1240 by the Vítkovci dynasty, is the second most extensive in the Czech Republic. The exquisite, completely preserved Baroque Chateau Theater, Baroque gardens, and a family of live bears at the Bear Moat are among the attractions of the complex.

Jindrichuv Hradec

Have you ever been betrayed in Jindrichuv Hradec? Well, the Jesuits and I have.

In the central square some four centuries ago a conflagration caught, and the Jesuit college was flaming high. The townspeople silently gathered and watched the fire without offering a helping hand.

Have you ever noticed what time does with personal stories in a historical town?

It remembers and gathers, it collects, but at the same time it melts them into a strange alloy.

Some extraordinary personal histories, acts of extreme passion and miracles, will not melt and will remain as domains of this special stockpile of genius loci. It is stored somewhere—maybe in old pavement and walls. Every perceptive pilgrim, in the middle of the night, as autumn fog rises above the river, or in morning rain, is aware of its existence, but the details must be read in old chronicles and records.

JINDRICHUV HRADEC

The district town of Jindrichuv Hradec has many remarkably well-preserved historic architectural examples of the Gothic, Renaissance and Baroque styles. Originating near the end of the 12th century, the village became a bustling town, and, In 1483, Prince Vladislav II elevated its status by adding two lions into the town's coat of arms and issuing a privilege of large markets. The earliest mention of the town's castle in the historical record was in 1220, when a nobleman, Jindrich I, lived at the manor that was located on the site. The castle complex *(opposite)* is the third largest in the Czech Republic and contains preserved remnants of 14th-century wall frescoes. The medieval castle was updated in the 16th century in the prevalent Renaissance style by Italian architects.

Jindrichuv Hradec (literally Henry's Castle) is a place with mystery hidden somewhere like a trout under a large stone in the river. The original dark medieval castle was enlarged into a playful Renaissance chateau, but the former heaviness rooted to the granite substrate endured. As I write these sentences, my heart is longing to walk again in night's darkness through the narrow lanes and bridges around the Castle; I wish to read the pictorial legend of St. George (1338) in the Castle or to listen to music in the large stucco-decorated round musical pavilion (or rondel) above the river. The musicians played in the lower floor and were heard through an oval orifice in the floor of the rondel, while aristocrats danced on the upper floor. Every age seems to have its own kind of Titanic, someone still dancing at an upper level in spite of the water rising down below.

CESKÉ BUDEJOVICE

Ceské Budejovice lies 100 miles south of Prague in the countryside of South Bohemia. The town's wide range of historic architecture dates from medieval times, including 13th-century houses, arcades, and the nearby castle of Hluboka. Remains of old fortifications can still be found in the former settlement around the Town Hall and Bishop's Palace. Near the old arsenal (built in 1531) stands the simply decorated Ceské Budejovice Salt House *(left)*. Famous for its Budvar Budweiser (no relation to American Budweiser), Ceské Budejovice's brewery exports their popular beer *(pivo)* to more than twenty countries around the world.

TREBON

The countryside surrounding Trebon *(right)* makes the area a popular destination for travelers with its many fishing lakes, healing peat bogs, woodlands and meadows. The town was founded in the mid-13th century. The expansive Trebon chateau, originally built for the powerful Rozmberk family, was renovated during the 16th century in the Renaissance style and contains the Town Archive, a collection of centuries-old books and manuscripts. Local people believe that the ghost of White Lady is still sometimes seen walking silently through the castle.

VILLAGE CHURCH IN SOUTHERN BOHEMIA *(below)*

Churches and taverns represented the two most important centers of any village, the former for communion with God, tradition and ancestors, and the latter as a center for gossip and for building and organizing the community.

CESKÉ BUDEJOVICE

At a small square in front of the Dominican monastery, you may read in the pavement: generations come, generations leave, but Earth remains.

Mystics and philosophers lived throughout southern Bohemia, but they kept their distance from Ceské Budejovice, a place of orderly burghers, petty bourgeoisie, where you built a house, sent your children to school and in the evening went to sleep. The horizontality of surrounding rivers and ponds creates a peaceful environment. It is nice to have a beer (original Budweiser, of course) at the large, sophisticated square. Do not miss the gentle curve of the square's pavement—it rises almost invisibly to a center where Samson's water fountain stands. But then return to tragic Krumlov, cold Prachatice or other places where beauty and pain will leave you wordless.

TREBON

When local poet Ladislav Stehlik writes about Trebon, he says that beauty was wandering through the world, but there she stopped.

Tiny Trebon's few streets, its square and chateau are encircled by large, artificial ponds created mostly in the 16th century. Thirty miles of the Golden Channel (itself a masterpiece of Renaissance technology) connected 200 ponds to give rise to fish farms that prosper to this day. Trebon carp is as much a part of Christmas supper in Bohemia as turkey is to an American Thanksgiving dinner.

The ponds were built in the locations of former marshes. The whole area was profoundly changed, but in a way that enriched the landscape. The pond Rozmberk, established in 1584, is the largest freshwater fishery in Europe. The pond covers 1200–1800 acres (depending on the water level) and is retained by a 1.7-mile-long dam that is 50–55 yards wide at the base. Eight hundred workers prepared the ground for the pond, and 700 lumberjacks cut trees for the dam construction. But the first dam was unstable and started to give way—another 1,600 people were called to work day and night to save the pond. During the high floods of 2002 when the town faced the danger of being wiped out by a single large wave from the pond, the four-century-old dams, strengthened by ancient oaks, withstood the pressure of as much water as was captured by the system of modern dams during the Vltava deluge! I stand in awe of both the workers' technical skills and bravery and the landscape they created, now protected as a UNESCO biosphere reserve.

TÁBOR

Tábor, a nice Renaissance town of curved streets and the Pilgrim's church of Klokoty where Our Lady appeared to children, is still an emotional place that divides the nation with the question of whether Hussites were bandits and murderers or fighters for a better world.

Tábor was created as a social Utopia and religious commune. Its history intertwines with the first major reformation movement that manifested in Europe.

Jan Hus was born, like so many reformers and religious philosophers, in the rather melancholic south Bohemian landscape. He soon recognized the abuses of the church, the papal schism (since 1378 there had been two, and later three, popes) and the too-worldly behavior of the Catholic church. Hus subscribed to an invisible church of brothers and sisters more than the visible church in Rome and considered the pope to be the Antichrist. He wanted to return to the Holy Scriptures as the sole source of Christian doctrine, rejecting later commentaries and papal decrees. In 1415, King Sigismund called a church council in Constance, Germany to find a solution for the papal schism. He invited Jan Hus, promising him safe conduct. But Hus was thrown into prison there and later burned at the stake as a heretic. He prayed loudly until engulfed by flames.

After Hus's death, many Bohemian nobles published a protest and offered protection to Hus's followers. Hussites broke ties with Rome and started to use a new liturgy in which Holy communion was given in both forms—bread and wine (instead of only bread). Conflicts between Catholics and Hussites become frequent—for example, in 1419, burghers were thrown from the windows of New Town Hall of Prague and were killed by a mob. The Hussites realized that they needed a military and spiritual base. They chose a location protected by the medieval castle Kotnov, and there they established Tábor. At the beginning, they built wooden walls and a church. Everyone placed his or her property into wooden barrels and from the beginning shared this common property. Tábor grew as farmers and townspeople from all over Bohemia joined this experiment in truth.

Defense was a constant concern. The military genius General Jan Zizka created a new system of using mobile wagon walls (a technique used later in the American west) as temporary forts. Hussites initiated the use of small firearms—they were called flutes or, in Czech, pístala, and the word survived as pistol.

Simple, often untrained, but impassioned Hussites were capable of driving away large, organized armies of enemies. However, their actions led to devastating civil war and unprecedented cruelties. Churches and monasteries were burnt down by Hussites as symbols of the decadent Catholic Church. Icons were destroyed, and their armies often traveled to Bavaria, or as far north as to the Baltic Sea, to steal wine and food.

This historical episode still divides Czech society. The Hussite movement is considered by many to represent one of the high points of Bohemian history. But the Hussites' sincere religiosity, self sacrifice, and attempts to right the church's wrongs must be weighed against their extreme cruelties, destruction of property, and the deterioration of the entire kingdom centuries later due to the Thirty Years War.

A century later Martin Luther initiated the Second Reformation with issues similar to those brought up by Hus. These movements eventually led to the departure of English Puritans on the Mayflower and their ideals continue in certain values that still characterize contemporary American society.

CULTURE AS A GENTLE MEANS OF SURVIVAL

*I wonder if I am qualified to write about Terezín,
because I did not suffer there. But part of the
responsibility of ensuring that the memory
will not fade away is mine.*

TEREZÍN AND LITOMERICE

The Labe (Elbe) River valley is a principal northern gateway to Bohemia from Germany. The steep, rocky canyon of the Labe north of Litomerice, close to Zernoseky where the tasty but dry north Bohemian wine is grown, is called in old chronicles *Porta Bohemica*. The place is marked by the three wooden crosses of Calvary mountain, which were erected at the acropolis of a huge prehistoric settlement. Salt from Saxony was transported on the river since at least the Bronze Age. A sequence of fortified places and salt stores was estab-

lished alongside the river, including two hills on which a walled Premyslid settlement was established at the end of the 9th century and, in the 13th century, the medieval town of Litomerice was founded. Its proximity to the northern border meant that in peaceful times the town prospered into a rich merchant center, but in wartime this border proximity brought the threat of total destruction. Litomerice is among the oldest Bohemian towns, but numerous conflicts have eliminated the medieval layer. Most of its preserved memorials date from Renaissance and Baroque times.

aged. The population dropped from 6,000 to less than 600, and still it was not the end of the story. Litomerice became an Archbishopric in 1655, and a Catholic seminary was established. Then, only a few decades later, new wars with Prussia began. Prussian Emperor Friedrich II spent a month here planning an invasion against Prague. The more recent history of nearby Terezín emerges from a setting already familiar with the tragic consequences of war.

But notice, please, something significant— how the arts and music soothe the suffering, how in the middle of wars some of the most peaceful statues were carved, the most tranquil pictures painted. To heal the wounds of such extensive suffering requires more than the dispositions of man alone.

Built as a fortress two miles south of Litomerice in the 1780s, Terezín was named after the Empress Maria Theresa. Invading armies did not waste their time besieging the powerful fortress, and it was never tested. A military prison existed here from the beginning. Some prominent prisoners kept here were the leader of the Greek uprising against the Turks, A. Ypsilanti, and Gavrilo Princip, the Serbian who triggered the First World War by assassinating Austrian Archduke Franz Ferdinand d'Este.

Terezín consists of two interconnected units: the large fortress with its enclosed town, and the small fortress (Malá pevnost), divided by the river Ohre. The river was diverted to flow under the fortress so its water could flood the main moat in only a few hours. The space between these two units was used to form marching formations. During the second world war, the small fortress operated as an interrogation prison for an international community of prisoners, partisans and resistance fighters, while the town became a Jewish ghetto.

In 1939 under German occupation, registration of all persons designated as Jews began. Their property was confiscated, their rights and social contacts restricted. They were forbidden to shop at normal stores, visit cinemas or libraries, use public transport, even to enter parks. After September 1941, they were also required to wear the yellow star of David. Systematic German machinery began to work on a plan called *Endlösung*,

Intolerance has plagued this area for centuries. In 1420, sixteen young men, followers of the reformer Jan Hus, were fetched out of the tower (later nicknamed the Tower of Disobedient Children) and drowned in the river. Zuzana Pichlová jumped into the river to share the watery deathbed with her lover.

During the next two centuries, the town prospered. Jewish merchants lived in the area close to the Dominican monastery. Boys were sent to Saxony to learn German, several lively international markets sold wares, the paintings of Lucas Cranach enriched local churches. But the town's strategic position brought disaster during the Thirty Years War, when the town was forced to defend itself against several passing armies. Of 597 houses in the town, only 93 survived undam-

TEREZÍN-TOWN AND LITTLE FORTRESS/MALÁ PEVNOST

Founded as a fortress by Emperor Joseph II in 1780 to keep the threat of Prussian invasion at bay, the walled town of Terezín was used by the National Socialist regime under Adolph Hitler as a propagandistic example of an "independent Jewish settlement." In November of 1941, under the Nazi occupation of Czechoslovakia (1939–1945), Theresienstadt, as it became known worldwide, was turned into a labor concentration camp during the widespread "Final Solution" campaign. Some 40,000 Jews from Prague alone were forced into the camp, along with more than 100,000 Jews from across Slovakia, Bohemia and Moravia. Most of the Jews sent to Terezín were eventually sent on to their deaths at Auschwitz. More than 60,000 suffered cruel deaths at Terezín itself due to overcrowding and torture. The original 18th-century small fortress, the Malá Pevnost, was used as a prison by the Nazis. Outside its walls is the National Cemetery for the Holocaust victims of Terezín. In memory of the thousands of Jews who perished here and elsewhere, the fortress is now a museum and National Memorial.

or Final Solution. Terezín was adapted to serve as a transit concentration camp before Jews were sent to extermination camps outside the Reich.

The first transport, called *Aufbaukommando*, or building commando, arrived in Terezín in November 1941. The next year, the remaining non-Jewish inhabitants of Terezín were moved out and the town was transformed into a prison. During the war, 150,000 prisoners passed through the camp; only 3,000 survived. Former military barracks housed the Jews. As many as 58,000 people were interned in the town at one time. Women and children were separated from the men and kept in special barracks. It was immensely overcrowded, with up to 400 people living in one room.

The whole town was controlled by a limited number of Nazis because every available soldier was needed on the Russian front. Everyday life was the responsibility of a Jewish council of elders. The indifference of the SS men helped to create extraordinary opportunities for cultural activity, despite Terezín's being a prison town. All concentration camps were about death and suffering, but Terezín was different—some families managed to stay together; lovers could sometimes secretly meet; a school was functioning. A children's magazine was illegally published, and a secret prayer room was established.

Terezín demonstrated during the Holocaust that culture is not merely a form of entertainment for the well fed, but also a gentle means of survival. The concentration camp occupants cre-

ated literary evenings, lectures, theater performances. Rafael Schächter conducted Verdi's *Requiem*, and Rudolf Franek debuted the children's opera, *Brundibár*. Fine artists were required to work in the building project office, but they smuggled out art supplies, which were used to create a collection of drawings expressing their secret emotions and suffering. Hundreds of these survived, hidden behind beams in Terezín's attics or immured in the walls. A local museum now displays these drawings in an intensely moving expression of the Terezín experience.

The last Nazi transport came in October 1944. The Allied front was approaching; the last SS men left on May 5th, 1945. Unfortunately, the liberation was marred by a typhus epidemic. This disastrous situation was managed by the Soviet Red Army. A quarantine was declared, and a town still full of thousands of people was transformed into a hospital. Deeds of bravery by the doctors and nurses who volunteered to help at Terezín were as common as death. In the next few weeks, the army managed to get the situation back under control, and the surviving former prisoners were finally able to return to their homes—in twenty-nine different countries.

A heavy, sad atmosphere still permeates the town. On my visits, I never fail to visit the secret prayer room and the railway. The end of the railway is the most poignant place in Terezín, where relatives came, family members departed for death in extermination camps, meetings and partings happened like ebbs of time.

CASTLES AND CHATEAUX BETWEEN HISTORY AND DREAMS

Ghosts are as common in castles as in chateaux, but castle ghosts are less civilized and they display rather an unpleasant sense of humor.

The central European space of Bohemia, Austria, Germany and other countries is extraordinarily rich in historical monuments. I have a list of 160 significant Bohemian prehistoric sites, 275 castles, about 340 chateaux and manor houses, 210 monasteries and a number of churches and historical buildings. When my friend, surrealist Martin Stejskal, once prepared a catalog of supernatural beings, ghosts and apparitions, he had to read 155 books of legends, and the list was still not complete. Some of the legends or fairy tales contain elements from the Bronze Age, and some motifs of folk songs and general folklore might predate even that period. Many villages around Prague are recorded in the 993 A.D. property list made by Brevnov monastery, and so may have more than one thousand years of history. I always feel paralyzed when challenged to summarize all this complexity in a few sentences or paragraphs.

Castles represent for many people the real essence of the Middle Ages: romantic tales associated with knights, battles, treasures and secrets. Romanticism is a cluster of attitudes and feelings that favors variety over uniformity, the infinite over the finite, nature over culture, freedom over limitations. Romantics prefer feelings to thoughts, emotion to calculation, intuition to intellect and night to day. In the modern age, many people seem to appreciate the anti-establishment and individualistic qualities of Romanticism. From this point of view, the recycled valor of medieval castles is still alive in the modern era.

Early medieval fortified places consisted of a moat, an earthwork fortification, a wooden palisade and a central tower that was called the keep or donjon. This tower had only a narrow entrance in the second floor, so when the castle courtyard was overrun, the last defenders could escape into the tower and withdraw the ladder. In central Europe, the evolution of castles occurred over only three centuries (c. 1230–1500), because castles became too small for larger military assemblages and because more precise and effective artillery was developed. Some castles grew into larger, more spacious structures known as chateaux, but a far greater number of Bohemian castles were deserted or destroyed to prevent bandits from settling there.

Prague Castle is, in fact, a chateau. The basic distinctions are as follows: the function of a castle was principally fortification. It was cold, its interior space was limited due to its massive defensive walls, and there was usually a limited water supply. It was born from a basic insecurity, and it was built primarily in the Gothic style. On the other hand, a chateau was large, and its purpose was to afford a pleasant life, social contacts, leisure and sometimes hunting activities. It was encircled by gardens, water was plentiful, and it tended to serve governmental or diplomatic rather than military purposes. Most chateaux were built during the Renaissance and Baroque periods, but historical styles of the 19th century were later common. The economic basis of a castle was usually a village, but behind a chateau you would find large farms, stables, barns and often a mill or brewery. A normal

castle had two circles of fortification, one or two towers, a small palace between them and some houses and bastions. The chateau was often built as a U-shaped palace. It sometimes contained a castle core or offices responsible for economic development of the area.

The gem among European castles is Karlstejn, but you must get into the parts that are not easily accessible to visitors—to the tower whose chapel is encrusted with semi-precious stones like jasper and amethyst, where Master Theodoric has painted a spiritual army of saints. The stones correspond to gems of Eternal Jerusalem described in the Apocalypse, the ceiling is covered by golden stars and the original windows are composed of gems in order to admit only the noble part of the light spectrum. Royal insignia and holy relics, including some of the most precious objects of Christianity, were kept here.

There are so many others. My most beloved castle is Krivoklat. It is full of life. In the center, you will find a Late Gothic chapel that remained for 500 years without any major changes. Hluboka chateau in southern Bohemia is a hunting lodge rebuilt in the 19th century in Tudor Gothic style. A famous gallery of Gothic and classical modern art is situated in its former stables. The beautiful eastern Bohemian town of

KARLSTEJN CASTLE/KARLSTEJN

King Charles IV built Karlstejn not for defensive purposes, but to house his collection of crown jewels and holy relics, choosing a low-profile site among higher hillocks so that it might be overlooked by enemies. Unlike most castles, it was constructed in one phase, built by French mason Matthew of Arras, and after his death, probably Petr Parlér, in 1348–1357. It was restored by Josef Mocker in the 19th century. The jewel-lined Chapel of the Holy Rood contains 127 panels painted by Master Theodoric in 1357–1365. The castle is in the central Bohemian district of Beroun.

Litomysl has a large Renaissance chateau, and there is a smaller chateau in Ploskovice, not very far from Litomerice. A pink chateau on the small island in Cervená Lhota is the charming setting for many films.

Recently, in winter, I was asked to be part of a group formed to help explore an old castle. The custodian was eager to find a secret room that was said to be located under a side tower. We climbed down, found a place that sounded hollow and finally broke into a low-lying passage. Unfortunately, it was a well-known conjunctive passage, but no one had ever realized that it was so close to the tower. As the day went on, we became closer to each other. The large, abandoned castle seemed to win some kind of influence over our minds. A story, full of uncertain allusions, slowly began to emerge: The

custodian resembles an old aristocrat. He lives with a young girl in the castle overlooking a small village, and he reads—as a glance into a pile of books on his table persuaded me—about black magic. He has strange dreams, and, were I in his place, I suppose my dreams would be unusual as well.

Once, in a dream, a specter came, shook him and slowly walked away. The custodian followed it, still dreaming, but the specter knocked on a certain spot of the castle wall and disappeared. In the morning, remembering his dream, the custodian went to the place and broke into the wall. He found there an immured old picture of the Madonna, which he showed to us. The picture was not very valuable, but it proved that local specters should be taken seriously.

But now, during this visit, he told us that he had the feeling that, in a secret room of the castle, there are dead bodies of prisoners who beg to be forgiven and buried. Such stories, pleasantly chilling when told in the security of our homes, are ominous in old, abandoned castles. I broke off contact and have never returned.

KRIVOKLÁT CASTLE/KRIVOKLÁT

Krivoklát, one of the oldest Bohemian castles, was established on a former Celtic-fortified hill as early as the 12th century, first as a small wooden hunting lodge and later as a more complex and significant royal castle. The castle has never been abandoned. Several Bohemian kings including Rudolf II lived here, and King Charles IV is said to have hunted for nightingales in the woods below the castle for his wife Blanca, who loved their songs. In Huderka, the castle's tower, the famous English alchemist Edward Kelley was imprisoned and broke a leg in an escape attempt. Some castles have the ambiance of a museum, of petrified history, but at Krivoklát, the past is as alive as a flower or tree.

SRBSKO

Nearby, a small village called Srbsko (literally, Serbia) is beautifully situated in an area of limestone caves containing archaeological remnants of several cultures. One of the oldest Central European Paleolithic artifacts, a hand axe, was found on the slopes of a steep canyon nearby.

PLOSKOVICE CASTLE

The earliest mention of Ploskovice *(above)* in the historical record was in the year 1057. Two hundred years later, the area around the early fortifications was controlled by the Order of Johannites by 1188. Architectural assessments estimate that a chateau was built on the site after the mid-1500s, when the property was mortgaged and taken from the Johannites. In the 17th century it passed into the hands of Anna Maria Francesca of the Lauenburg House, wife of Duke Gaston de Medici, and the castle's final construction phase was then completed. The Baroque palace became property of the Hapsburg rulers in the early 19th century, and for a time was the family seat of Ferdinand I until 1848 when it became a Czech National monument.

BOZENA NEMCOVA

Prominent Czech writer Bozena Nemcová was born in Prague's Malá Strana, rumored to be the illegitimate child of a noble aristocratic family. She was young and beautiful when she married Jan Nemec in 1837; she still played with dolls. Her husband, a customs official, was reportedly possessive and extremely jealous of his delicate and intelligent wife. He belonged to an active group of Czech patriots and Nemcová quickly found herself in the center of the Czech national revival. Although she had little formal education, she worked hard to earn a place in the world of literature and science.

Soon she was involved in writing novels. She pursued activities such as collecting folk tales, a sort of cultural anthropology.

Her personal life was a series of disasters. Misunderstood by her husband, she had several lovers, but most of her relationships ended in disillusionment. She led the life of an independent woman at a time when such a position was totally unthinkable among the middle classes. Desperate, sick and often hungry, Nemcová ran away in 1853 to Litomysl *(opposite)* to write a book, entitled *Grandmother*, but she became destitute after the publishers stopped paying her for the manuscript. Her husband found her near death and brought her home, where she died on January 21, 1862 at about 43 years of age. The country mourned her passing.

Grandmother, the most beautiful and idyllic book she ever wrote, was in fact conceived in the times of profound personal crisis that could be overcome only by her memories of a happy village childhood. Nemcová is a heroine, an angel of Czech literature. The mixture of shining beauty and black despair, her bright intelligence against the dullness of conventional society is still so familiar to her readers. Most of her contemporaries are now fossilized in books that no one opens, but Nemcová is beloved; reading her novels brightens our lives. Like Emily Dickinson, she seems not to belong to any sphere that society could accept and no world we really know.

LITOMYSL

The town of Litomysl in eastern Bohemia is the birthplace of many Czech cultural personalities, most notably the famous composer Bedrich Smetana (1824–1884). The sgraffito-decorated Renaissance chateau, built for Vratislav of Pernstejn in the 16th century, owns the old brewery where Smetana was born. It has been restored to the appearance it had in the 19th century, when the Smetana family lived in the quarters. Since the early 19th century, this area has been at the forefront of the Czech national revival. The annual Festival of Opera and Classical Music lures highly acclaimed musicians and audiences from all over the world. The chateau was built on the site of a 10th century Slavic fortified settlement which guarded the merchant route to Moravia. The building, including a small but well-preserved historical theater, was recently listed as a UNESCO monument.

A FLUID MOSAIC
THE CENTRAL EUROPEAN
LANDSCAPE

In both the classic agricultural and mountainous regions of Europe, however deserted and natural the place may seem, nature is somehow overprinted with a human aura. A constant high voltage contradiction between the patient constructive diligence of farmers and a nullifying tendency of newcomers and intruders seems to be the basic theme of European history.

The Central European landscape is characterized by the contrast between an ancient relief of gently undulating hills that developed since the Mesozoic age, and the sharp edges of river valleys and young mountain chains of the Tertiary and Quaternary age. Two landscapes are characteristically mixed together: soft agricultural plains and hard, rocky ridges.

Although the contemporary mid-European landscape has a prehistoric basis, it is primarily the result of the medieval revolution of the second half of the 13th century, when more than ninety percent of all towns and villages were established and were connected by roads we still use. The countryside was divided into three levels: the largest and lowest part of the landscape belonged to fields, the bases of hills were occupied by pastures, and the hills with their rocky soils were covered by forest. Thus, the basic plan of the landscape was already drawn seven centuries ago and has remained relatively unchanged until recently.

The fine texture of the European landscape is noticeable—villages are characteristically located two to four miles apart, and every thirty miles or so you get into a different landscape with a different group of people and subtle distinctions of culture and food.

The traditional European village or town has a pyramidal silhouette that reflects the community's values. The highest point belongs to the church tower. The second in height is usually the town hall, then the burghers' houses. Building height diminishes to the lesser houses at the outskirts, then comes the city wall or the ring of gardens. The edge of the town or village was in the past sharply defined, because agricultural land was required for food production and was very expensive.

Mining activities and glass and iron production have since the 16th century considerably changed the landscape. The virgin forest disappeared, replanted with either spruce or a more natural mixed deciduous forest. However, the development and growth of the past few decades have affected the character of the land more than the several previous centuries. For many Europeans, this landscape change represents almost a tragedy. They feel so rooted in their soil that the landscape has become part of their identity—change the landscape and they lose a part of their soul.

74

THREE TYPES OF LANDSCAPES

Danish architect Christian Norberg-Schulz, in his book *Genius Loci*, developed an elementary division of landscapes. In classical landscape, such as in hilly agricultural lands, the forces of nature and man are in balance and enrich each other. In romantic landscapes, as in mountains, the forces of nature are wild, uneven and stimulating. In cosmic landscapes, such as in lowlands or desert, the sky is big, the cosmos overwhelming. Each phase of the human life needs a different landscape. A young person thrives in the adventure of the exciting romantic landscape. Mature people need to live and raise their children in a classical landscape where you can swim in a pond, safely enjoy the forest, observe animals at a farm. Meditative personalities seek tranquil, open spaces where noble ideas crystallize in the orbits of sparkling stars and can freely rise up to unknown spheres.

CELTIC SANCTUARY/ KELTSKA SVATYNE

This abandoned and forgotten Celtic site, surrounded by farmland, is one of the Viereckschanzen or rectangular rims. It is a roughly square sanctuary with sides about 100 yards long. No archaeological research was conducted here, but other such sanctuaries sometimes contain a holy well, where wooden images of Celtic gods are buried, and a small temple. Here one may dream of the gods rising above the green meadow from the nether world.

AN UNKNOWN THIRST

The visitor wants to see and maybe to learn, but the pilgrim wants to be changed. The word pilgrim appears in medieval manuscripts and describes a devoted person who travels to sacred places...How many types of sacredness do we know—a mountain, a monastery, a flower, or even water emerging from unknown depths or an unusually shaped rock? Is a place an answer to an unknown thirst inside?

HOLY MOUNTAIN/SVATÁ HORA
The district town of Pribram was an important silver mining center, and in 1875, a record depth of three thousand feet was reached in a mine. Uranium mining occurs here today. Pribram is located forty miles southwest of Prague, and besides a mining museum, a castle and preserved industrial architecture, you can visit Svatá Hora, a place of pilgrimage since the 13th century, located next to a miraculous spring with highly radioactive water. During the 15th and 16th centuries, a sanctuary was built to house the adored statuette of Our Lady. Legend holds that a reclusive guardian of the sanctuary, Jan Procházka, was healed of his blindness in the summer of 1632. Shortly after, the Holy Mountain sanctuary was given to the Jesuit Order, which held the site until 1773. They built the present Baroque sanctuary, dedicated to the Assumption of Our Lady, in 1673. Two hundred covered steps lead up the hill to the pilgrimage site.

STONES OF MEMORY

In some regions of central Europe, one finds strange, often coarse and uneven crosses that seem more likely to have been created by some playful (or possibly dark) natural force than by a man: They are rough and unprofessional, made of unpolished sandstone or granite. Some bear strange marks—letters; sometimes pictograms of a sword, axe, female figure or sun circle—but more often they silently offer a message without clues.

They are heavy, massive. One is aware of their intensity, as though they were stories that were turned into stone and then forgotten in a field or crossing of the road.

Cemeteries were called holy fields, and the dead resembled seeds buried into the Earth, maternal Earth touched by generations of farmers, tamed soil. But if someone was buried alone outside the area of living people, he or she could have been a heretic, a murderer, a stranger. Some tragedy, something unusual and thus dangerous, could be sensed around these individual crosses.

So these crosses, known as crosses of reconciliation or of peace, or even as propitiatory crosses, became a focus of local ghost stories: small fires may appear around them in the darkness; unknown voices may ask some unusual question. Horses dislike these sites.

What do we know about them? The oldest ones that we are able to date are from the Gothic era of the 14th and 15th centuries, but some of them, archaic and primitive but still full of vague recollections, may have come from even earlier times. The most recent ones were erected at the end of the 18th century, or sometimes even later. We do not know much about their purpose. Most of these crosses are associated with some ancient tragedy, with a place where someone was killed accidentally or even murdered, where lights appeared or voices were heard around midnight.

The instrument of death is often depicted on the stones—knife, sword, axe. Some fairy tales and some real stories (e.g., about a hunter killed there by poachers, about a girl who fell under bewildered horses or an overturned carriage)

are recorded. Other stories explain that a person who deliberately or accidentally killed someone had to make a rough, heavy cross and, for the sake of mind and salvation, bring it to the place where the accident happened, maybe just for reflection and penitence of a bad deed, or perhaps to dissolve the dark atmosphere or to calm down the spirits of the dead, who are sometimes so hungry...

We know of more than 1,700 such crosses in the Czech area, and several thousand others are located in Austria, Germany and elsewhere. In spite of their number, tourists and even local visitors seldom see them: abandoned in the landscape, neglected in corners and behind the walls of village churches, they are too rough to belong to the realm of art, and sometimes they do not even seem to belong to the realm of institutionalized religion. An informal group initiated an intensive search for these crosses in 1984. Researching copper-etched maps, reading village chronicles and talking to old people, they gathered documentation, stories, old agreements concerning the conditions of how the death could be repaid, how one could ask for mercy and salvation even when an innocent life was lost. The task still goes on, and every year new crosses are discovered in overgrown shrubs or embedded in ancient, crumbling walls.

The cross shown here is hidden between two hills close to Kutná Hora. An important intersection of several mining roads is located close to the cross. Silver mines dating to the 14th, 15th, and 16th century open their deep shafts nearby. One feels some discomfort there, immersed in old, fearful histories. The cross does not add much optimism. It seems to be saying: stop for a while, pray for the victims of unknown crimes...but do not linger long.

SANCTUARIES

Two types of sanctuaries, or sacred centers for ritual and worship, are recognized in cultural anthropology: cave sanctuaries and sanctuaries located at the tops of hills. Cave sanctuaries belong to your own roots. They signify that inner space where, if you go deep enough, you will have to fight, like the hermit Ivan, with demons. You are alone there and your individual salvation is at stake, but being close to your roots, you are at the spring of your inner strength. But visiting sanctuaries at the top of mountains, you are not alone. You embrace the landscape and other people, moving from your inner space to a shared space where the fate of the community is at stake. In the cave, you focus inward, but at the top of the mountain, you dissolve your separate self. Contraction and expansion, the breath of life. In your life, there are periods when you have look to within to discover strength, and periods when you ascend to some basic unity, grace and beauty.

THE MONASTERY OF SVATÝ JAN

From the Church of St. John, you enter the second, underground chapel in a former cave that was enlarged by the monks. You kneel at the stone where, according to a legend, the hermit Ivan prayed, placing your forehead on the small depression in the stone to become unified with the touch of St. Ivan and so many pious pilgrims. And then, in the cave, you sense the underground spring beneath your feet, and you notice the opening in the ceiling of the limestone space where a demon, fighting with the hermit, broke through the ceiling. You are touched; you start to understand the story in your heart. You know that the story has changed over the years, but still you are aware of some basic truth of the place. Genius loci is powerful here.

The monastery of Svaty Jan, which includes the Church of St. John under the Rock, is just twenty miles southwest of Prague, built into Bohemian karst. It is situated under a steep limestone cliff where, directly under the cross at the top of the mountain, the orifice of a large cave can be observed. Few places outside Prague have so captured the imagination of Bohemia's poets and writers during the past four hundred years. Here, kings and emperors dwelt, early Renaissance scientists observed the formation of stalagmites and stalactites in a nearby cave, writers of Baroque legends composed their verses about wise and bearded hermits, 19th-century writers tried to revive past glory. Even as late as the 20th century, Bohumil Hrabal located a part of his famous novel *I Served the King of England* here. After the 1948 Communist coup d'état, the monastery was transformed into a prison for capitalist millionaires.

But it was more than a thousand years ago that the hermit Ivan discovered here a cave with an underground spring. He settled here in the fear of God, according to a legend, for forty years. As early as the 11th century, a chapel was established in the cave for the baptism of pagans. Later, Benedictine monks arrived and established beside the cave a secluded monastery that grew larger during the Hussite wars, even as other monasteries were being destroyed. The monastery became a pilgrimage site after the discovery of St. Ivan's relics in the 16th century.

RÍP MOUNTAIN

In the middle of an ancient, fertile settlement area between central and northern Bohemia, where the continuity of prehistoric cultures is the longest, an isolated volcanic mountain called Ríp resembles the breast of Mother Earth. It is the place where the father of all Czechs climbed the hill, talked to the gods and decided to settle his tribe.

The small Romanesque rotunda of St. George stands at the top of Ríp Mountain, but no older prehistoric relics have been found there. The place, being the only hill in the area, would have been extremely desirable for a fortified settlement, but the lack of archaeological finds suggests that Ríp was, like some ancient Olympia, dedicated to gods, not men.

In any archaic culture, we consistently encounter the concept of axis mundi, or the axis of the world. Everything has a center, whether a person or a landscape; landscape is just another type of being. Through our center we pass into other worlds.

Just imagine a standing person, tower of a church, tree of life or sacred mountain. Their roots go into the underworld to the realm of the dead, with the central part—the nave of a church or trunk of a tree of life—staying in this world and this community, but their branches or towers reach the heavens. The center is the axis of communication.

It is likely that the mountain Ríp has, for many civilizations, represented the sacred axis of the world, irresistibly attracting the eye and provoking an acknowledgment of the sacred. You want to bow with reverence toward this mountain.

HE WILL BE CALLED BY NAME WHEN FISH WILL SWIM IN THE CATHEDRAL.

– adoration by a Czech poet

Is it a feeling of a different, cyclic time? Is it the feeling of sacredness? Do we need to have contact with Great Memory, with its sum of previous experiences, fates, tears and accomplishments of generations past? Has Death been banished from our lives, or do we long to touch some basic quality of life as rough as wood or stone? Do we have a natural soul that yearns for the natural elements such as ocean, animals or thunder; and at the same time a cultural or social soul that longs after eternal but changing social forces? Do we need to enter a River of Culture that flows through European landscape from a Paleolithic age tens of thousands of years ago?

The reasons we visit and return to historical places deserve consideration. Beyond the obvious beauty of the art of previous ages, there may be other reasons. Being no islands, we need to be connected to art, history and nature like knots on an ancient Oriental carpet. Historical places help us live more than one life. They evoke feelings from the depths of shared collective memory. Places are like mirrors and give us a new awareness of ourselves. Continually confronted with the mixture of sacredness, beauty, suffering and death, we realize that there is more than just one culture. We want to belong to this never-ending story.

Ships are safe in the harbor, but that is not what ships were built for, according to a sign that I read on the door of a church. Heave the anchor! Travel, read, seek, and if you are lucky you will hear the echoes of voices that will still sound when fish swim in the cathedral.